SHORT STORIES OF MODERN TIMES PAST

A.L. KING

ISBN-13: 9798695521429
ISBN-10: 1477123456

Cover design by: Art Painter
Library of Congress Control Number: 2018675309
Printed in the United States of America

CONTENTS

THANK YOU FOR READING

If you would like to receive **FREE & EXCLUSIVE** content on up-coming stories by A.L. KING, please follow our social media pages and join our mailing list below. Thanks again for reading!

Website: authoralking.wordpress.com
Facebook: authoralking3
Instagram: @a.l.king3
Twitter: @AuthorALKING3
Email: authoralking3@gmail.com

INTRODUCTION

"History repeats itself until we learn the lessons that we need to change our path."

-dailythoughts.arvindkatoch.com

THE ROCK, THE MARNE, AND THE SOLDIER'S HEART

"Company, attention! Rock of The Marne Sir."

"Carry on."

"Rock of The Marne Sir!"

We all yelled as our company commander walked by our platoon. We were up at the butt crack of dawn each day to get ready to do PT (physical training). *Rock of the Marne* is our credence or greeting while in basic training here in Fort Benning Georgia. We also use **Hough** or **Hooah** for greetings and salutations here as well. It's like saying *yeah* or *you understand* or *great* when speaking with fellow soldiers. It is an expression of acknowledgement, excitement, agreeance, and exuberance for the most part.

"You going to the shopette?"

"Hooah!"

"You hungry?"

"Hooah!"

"You can't suck this bad at running 2 miles Private! Hooah?!"

"Hoooaaah Drill Sergeant!"

You know, stuff like that... But we represent the *3rd Infantry Division* in Fort Stewart Georgia, which is a few hours away. If I remember correctly, the saying "Rock of the Marne" came from the defense set up by the 3rd Division at *The Marne River*. This occurred during a change in the tide of *World War I*, while the troops were serving in France. They essentially changed the course of the war, and I am proud to be a part of their great legacy! My name is Rick Myers, but everyone calls me Ricky, or Myers here. I am a Private in the United States Army. I left for the Military when I was 18 years old (I am currently 19), so almost right out of high school. I had a job at the shipyard for a year or so before that. But I barely made it through my senior year, due to getting involved with the wrong crowd. I got into trouble with the law because of it. Thankfully, I only received misdemeanor charges that were all dropped. My recruiter telling the judge that I recently enlisted in the Army was enough to show that I was serious about making a change. My MOS (Military Occupational Specialty) is an 11B, or 11 Bravo infantryman. The amazing Rachel Dawson, who is the love of my life, is patiently waiting on the other side for me after I graduate bootcamp and AIT (Advanced Individual Training). Our training is also known as *One Station Unit Training* (OSUT) here in Fort Benning. This is due to our basic training and AIT being combined for infantrymen and other combat specialties. Hopefully, I get to see her on family day and before I head out to my permanent duty station. She said she may not be able to make it to our family day celebration due to work and limited vacation hours. She is one of the main reasons why I enlisted and why I want to make a better life for us and our future family. She is my high school sweetheart and a part of my destiny. My kindred spirit, and the Yin to my Yang... Yep, That's Rachel! We don't have phone privileges here unless it's an emergency, but we have been communicating through letters via first class mail. Everyone seems to be doing well back home in the great state of Virginia.

Now I was a star athlete in high school and Prom King, so I was pretty popular in school. Being the starting quarterback of the JV and Varsity football teams, it was easy for me to get caught up in the wrong things: drugs, alcohol, bullying, sleeping around, had my interest until I met Rachel, and that all changed. She helped me stay focused on what really mattered, my future. And though I was offered a full ride scholarship to Virginia Tech to play football, I decided to go into the military for a chance to serve my country. Rachel fussed me out for choosing this career path, but I wanted the full soldier experience. You know, I wanted to see what it was like to be a soldier who fights for our freedom! There is this one thing I forgot to mention earlier... I have a mild case of aortic stenosis, which is a heart condition that restricts the blood flow from your heart to your main artery, better known as the aorta. I've had it since birth, which is rare, but it has not really impacted my life that much apart from feeling weak and fatigued at times. I kind of look at it as a superpower that enables me to push myself beyond the limits of a normal human being. That may be the comic books talking though... I was able to get a waiver to enlist into the military due to the severity of my case. Rachel and my family worry about me putting my body through too much stress by joining the Army. But I told them like I told my football coach back in high school, I got this!

After running like derby horses for an hour, we made it back from PT. I can easily run 2 miles under 12 minutes, but I'm working with my battle buddy Clifton Jones to get him ready for our upcoming PT test. We also have our field exercise coming up, which is the last thing we need to complete before moving on to the next phase of our training. Not sure what the details are surrounding it, but we should know more the day of.

"Hey Cliff, how you feeling man?"

"Man, I feel like my heart is about to pop out of my chest, slap me in the face, and say... why do you hate me so much?!" He said as we both started cracking up.

"Yeah I hear you, this PT is pretty rigorous, and you being a lineman when you played football, doesn't help that much."

"Who you telling... Our coaches set us up for failure... Instead of saying eat fatty foods and keep your weight up, they should have said pick up this lettuce wrap and diet cucumber water to stay fit! You know, every now and again. All those double mega cheeseburgers with a diet soda, didn't help my cause at all! I stay having the meat sweats dude!"

"You're a fool Cliff," I said as we were still laughing out loud.

"Let's go get some chow, we got a long day ahead of us Hooah."

"Hooah, you don't have to tell me twice!" Cliff said as we made our way to the chow hall.

So, whether the setting is high school, a 9 to 5 job, or even basic training, there's always a hotshot that wants to show everybody up. Julian Rodgers is that guy! He's in Charlie Company and they think they're big stuff! We were cool at first, but then he set me up to get smoked by one of the Drill Sergeants. Julian was behind me and pushed the person in front of me as a prank. The person thought it was me and pushed me for it. Of course I pushed them back, and we both had to do mountain climbers and flutter kicks until we reached muscle failure. Since I'm a squad leader, which I thought was an awesome privilege, I had to get smoked in front of my platoon. However, my platoon had to get smoked along with me, so that wasn't beneficial for anyone... My squad definitely cursed me out about it later that day. I think my Drill Sergeant picked me to be squad leader because I was a QB in high school and could ace my PT test. We were in Bravo Company and known as **The Dragons.** I think other platoons were jealous of us because we had a reputation of being the best platoon on the base. But, from that day forward, I've calmed down some, even though I still thought of ways to get him back. And blanket parties are a real thing; not just something you see in movies like *Full Metal Jacket,* by Stanley Kubrick. One of my all-time faves by the way. He had me feeling like "Gomer Pyle" that's for sure... This was something I thought about doing, but he's in another company and has an entourage who probably wouldn't let that happen. Plus, I don't want to set a bad example for my squad. I'll just have to let it go for now...

"Hey, how are you unworthy degenerates doing today?!" Julian said as he made his grand entrance into the chow hall.

"Shut up Julian!" One of the other soldier's said.

"Yeah sit down somewhere!" Said another soldier.

Julian loved being the center of attention anywhere he went. Whether it was singing cadence, or leading marches, he had to be in the forefront of it all! I wasn't going to give him the satisfaction that day.

"Whatever! You know you guys suck and can't hang with the best right?! Oh yeah, if you haven't heard, if any of you losers fall out of the final road march to the field site, you'll lose your family day, so you best step your game up!" He said as he went to sit down with his cronies.

Was that true? Would I lose my family day if I fell out of the road march? I did hear from one of the other classes that it was extremely far, and even the most athletic or fit soldiers fell out... I can't worry about that now, I have to see the love of my life, so I'll make it no matter what! Wakeup call was typically 4:30am and lights out was 2100 hours or 9:00pm which was cool. Waking up before the roosters crowed wasn't though. We were all like vacuous zombies traipsing around until our Drill Sergeant yelled at us to "get the move on private," or "toe the freaking line," or my personal favorite, "half right, face!" You knew a Drill Sergeant meant business when they said that... It was all in a southern drawl too, which sounded cool, but was even more intimidating. They did have their comical moments though. Like this one time, we had a battle buddy who could not find the azimuth on their map in our "Land Nav" course. The Drill Sergeant told them to get their head out of their *fourth point of contact* so they could see straight and called them *private butthead* from that point on. We tried our best not to laugh as we feared we would get smoked if we did... But it was lights out and Cliff and I were bunk mates, so you know we barely got any sleep talking and telling jokes all night.

"Hey Ricky, how do you feel about tomorrow bro?" Cliff said with a sense of uncertainty in his voice.

"I don't know man, I'm nervous because I don't want the added pressure of knowing our family day could be taken away from us if we fallout of the march."

"Well, you don't have anything to worry about. I'm sure those chicken legs are going to carry you the distance hahaha." He said as we tried to keep our laughter down.

"Yeah, I've skipped leg day a time or two in my life. You just make sure you get your grizzly bear looking self over the finish line." I said as everyone started to listen in on our little roast session.

"Ok, I'm going to start calling you chicken little with your malnourished toothpick legs. You need some milk for your legs and your lumpy hairline. You look like the *Toxic Avenger*. Someone get this man a mop and a tutu!"

The whole barracks was cracking up now and once you get Cliff on a roll, it's hard for him to stop. But I think I have the mic drop punchline next. And we all look like the **Toxic Avenger** with lumpy shaved heads for basic training, so that joke was lame... Ok maybe it was a little funny, but now it's time to end this...

"You know what Cliff, if you take your ginormous head, Thomas's ears, and Eugene's nose and put it all together, you'll have a special edition Mr. Potato Head doll!" I said as everyone busted out laughing.

Cliff was laughing too, but then started booing me to drown out the laughter from our platoon.

"I love you man, never forget that. After training is all said and done, make sure you keep in touch ok? And we should all get matching tats. How cool would that be to have a dragon shooting flames to rep the squad?!" Cliff said changing the vibe of the room.

"I knew you were just a soft cuddly teddy bear. Don't get all emotional on me now. It's not like we are going to war or won't see each other again. And matching tattoos may be a bit much don't you think? But I got you bro, and I love you too." I said as we started to calm down and get focused on the task at hand.

The day of the field exercise was here. Everyone from my company or platoon was ready for action! My buddy Cliff even passed his PT test with flying colors and did his 2-mile run in 14 minutes! Our Drill Sergeant finally revealed, we would be marching roughly 24 miles to and from the field site. We've done a few mock road marches, 12 miles at least, but not 24 miles with 40 pounds of equipment in our rucksack... that's crazy! I was a little worried at that moment. I did receive a letter from my folks saying they would be there for family day, but my heartbeat, Rachel, said she may not be there due to work. Either way, I have to believe she will be there, and use the thought of her as my motivation! Our company was broken up into different groups, one on each side of the road. There was also an ambulance in the middle of the road, trailing behind us. This was just in case one of us fell out or needed medical attention. As we were making our way towards the field site, I put my earplugs in to help tune out the noise surrounding us. This also helped me get into my zone and keep a steady pace. We took turns singing cadence and joked about our next duty assignment after training. Roughly 10 miles into the road march, my legs started to cramp up and I started to fall back in the ranks. My heart started to flutter which was new and concerning. We stopped every so often to drink water and rest, but the weight of my rucksack and the pace in which we were moving, started to take its toll. The sweltering Georgia heat didn't help either.

"Don't fall out Private! If you do, you'll lose your family day!" My Drill Sergeant yelled.

Now I don't know if he was serious or not, but I wasn't going to take that chance. I thought about my love Rachel, I thought about seeing my family, I thought about General Joseph Dickman, and the *38th Infantry Regiment* leader, Colonel Ulysses McAlexander. They wouldn't give up the fight, and they sacrificed so much... I have to keep going! I am a warrior; I am a soldier, and I shall remain! As I started to climb back up into the ranks, my chest began to tighten, and my breath became labored. I've never felt this discomfort before... Was my heart condition worsening? Do I need to fall out and take the ambulance the rest of the way? These thoughts started racing through my mind as I noticed Julian starting to fall back as well. Now I could be a jerk and let him miss out on family day, but it's not about me at this point. It's about our code of honor and never leaving a battle buddy behind. As I made my way to Julian, I started to lose my breath even more and started feeling sharp pains in my chest. My Drill Sergeant noticed me wincing and asked me if I needed medical attention, and if I needed to get in the ambulance for further evaluation. He even shouted at me to get in. But I told him that I was good and pushed through the pain. At that moment, I heard a voice say, "don't quit, you were made for this." It was strange... as the voice seemed to be audible and not in my head... I looked up, but no one was there. I only saw the soldiers in the road march, and my Drill Sergeant who was focused on cursing someone else out. But I finally reached Julian in hopes of motivating him to get back in the ranks.

"Hey man, you're going to make it!" I said as Julian's head dropped towards the ground.

"I don't know Myers; this is harder than I expected. We still have a lot of miles left before we make it to the field site. There's no way I'm going to make it!" He said with defeat in his voice.

"You can do it! Just put your earplugs in, think about the latest song you love or your girl back home. Let that be your motivation! I'll be your pace setter, just keep up!"

"Dude your nuts! I set you up and you're still trying to help me? Why?"

"Well for one, I'm not petty like you, and for two, we're wearing this uniform that represents something bigger than any petty beef we could have."

As he laughed and agreed with what I said, we both started to move up in the ranks. Before we knew it, we were at the field site! And though we could barely stand up straight, due to our legs cramping violently, we cried tears of joy and perspiration once we crossed the finish line! We also celebrated because we would get to see our loved ones on family day! My chest was tight, and I still had slight pain in my left arm, but I couldn't drop out and let Rodgers and my family down...

Once we made it to the site, we were tasked to set up our tents, dig foxholes, and set up our perimeter at camp. We trained to simulate live war time scenarios for our field exercises. We had to take our M4 rifle, TA-50 (Army-issued Individual Gear), Kevlar helmet, flak vest, and protective mask with us everywhere we traveled. I remember when we had to go to the gas chamber. I told Cliff not to eat heavy that morning. He upchucked all his breakfast after we left the gas chamber. I would have laughed if I could see straight, but the CS gas had us all choking and gasping for air. Yeah, not a good experience, memorable, but terrible to say the least. Our anti-aircraft training was awesome though! We had to low crawl for a mile in the mud under barbwire while they shot munitions above our heads. We also did infantry training that dealt with tactical movements, extraction, and infiltration of enemy territory. We even had laser tag gear and blanks that we used to simulate live combat scenarios. We had a blast with that!

After we completed our combat exercises, we held a preliminary graduation ceremony at a river site that symbolized the battle at "The Marne River." I couldn't help but shed more tears when they played *God Bless the U.S.A.* A song by Lee Greenwood. Not everyone in our company or battalion made it, but thankfully myself, Julian, and my battle buddy Cliff did! He outpaced us for most of the march! We will forever be changed by this experience... It showed us that we could accomplish anything we put our hearts and minds to do. Being a soldier in the military, regardless of which branch you choose to serve in, creates a bond that cannot be broken by difference in opinion, race, creed or culture. Our pledge and oath are bigger than us. It's about ensuring we represent our country, flag, and constitutional rights with integrity and honor in our free world! It's about looking out for our fellow brothers and sisters to ensure no one is left behind during challenging times... That night, I felt like I finally understood why God put me on this earth. Not just to be a soldier that fights for our freedom, but to make a difference in the world and the lives of others. Also, to stand against social injustices which disregard our rights, and overlooks our equality as human beings. After the ceremony concluded, we began to make our way back to the barracks. We didn't have to walk as far this time as we rode back in an FMTV (Family of Medium Tactical Vehicles) after the halfway mark.

Family day was finally here! We got to spend time with our family the entire weekend since we would be staying here several more weeks to complete the rest of our training. I saw my mom, dad, and brother in the crowd. We had to be at attention and stoned faced the whole time until we were released, but I did see them! I was also scanning the crowd for Rachel but didn't see her anywhere. After the ceremony, my parents and brother came up to me and gave me a big hug. They all shed tears and were overwhelmed with how proud they were in that moment. Needless to say, I cried again but blamed it on the dust in the field.

"Hey stranger, long time no see... You just going to stand there or are you going to turn around and show me some love?!"

Wait, I know that voice and that sarcasm...

"Rachel?!"

My angel, my rock, my heart, she made it! I embraced her, lifted her off the ground, and spun her around like they do in those cheesy romantic movies you see. I guess they weren't lying about that either... Oh, and I planned on proposing to her at family day, hence my concern when she said she may not make it. My brother and parents knew about it and had the ring. A shiny rock that I've been saving up for since my senior year in high school. After telling my little brother Michael to close his eyes, we passionately kissed as time stopped around us. I couldn't have been happier in that moment! Michael or Mikey as we call him, handed me the ring as I got on one knee in front of everybody!

"Rachel, you are perfection to me. You believed in me when no one else did. I knew from the very first time we met, that we would be in this moment where I ask for your hand in marriage. You are the love of my life and my desire to live. Will you marry me?" It was silent for a moment, and by this time, everyone including my Drill Sergeants were watching.

"Well I guess, since you put me on the spot and all... Just kidding. Of course I'll marry you Ricky! I love you more than life!" She said as we both started to cry, and everyone cheered.

This was definitely a hallmark moment and the best day of my life! According to some of my teachers and numerous haters in high school, I wasn't supposed to be here. I was supposed to be somewhere messing up my life, or worse; however, I'm glad and fortunate that the narrative changed! I've accomplished more than I could ever dream of so far in my life! I know there is a lot more to experience on this journey, but the faith that I have, and the strength of my heartbeat, Rachel, is more than enough to keep me marching on! **Rock of the Marne!** Salute!

THE ROCK, THE MARNE, AND THE SOLDIER'S HEART: PART II

Trigger Warning:

Though most of this story is fictional, some of the events that take place are based on actual events that occurred during the attacks that happened on

September 11th, 2001. The story also deals with the Afghanistan and Iraq war that followed. If you are a civilian, soldier, or veteran who suffers from PTSD, please read this story with caution. Thank you.

September 11th, 2001

It was a dreary Tuesday morning in Fort Benning Georgia... We all just finished PT and it was about 9am. It was unusually chilly that morning for September, but the chill of the air was still on our uniforms as we watched the TV in disbelief. We all gathered in the day room; NCOs (Non-Commissioned Officers), Officers, and Privates alike. We watched in terror as these tragic events unfolded before our eyes. That fateful morning where four commercial airplanes were highjacked by an Islamic terrorist group known as *Al-Qaeda* and flown into historic buildings killing hundreds of innocent people... *The Twin Towers* of the *World Trade Center, The Pentagon*, and a field in rural Pennsylvania, were the monuments or areas primarily damaged in this horrific catastrophe. There was a myriad of emotions felt after an unsettling silence pierced the atmosphere as we all stood there frozen in shock. There were tears, sympathy, anger, and rage that permeated the room. We gasped as we watched people jump from the towers to escape the burning debris; the screams we heard, the chaos, the fire and carnage while the buildings collapsed, it was all extremely hard to watch. After what seemed like hours of silence and despair, our 1st Sergeant looks around the room and says, **Well, get ready to go to war**...

Some cheered at his statement, while others seemed a bit shaken up by it. Either way, we were ready to do what we had to do to fight, and I wanted revenge... This is what I signed up for. To fight for our country against enemies, domestic and abroad. I thought about my soon to be wife and family back in the 7 cities of Virginia. Thought about how they must be feeling seeing this nightmare unfold right in front of us. I'm Rick Myers by the way. I go by Myers or Ricky by my battle buddies, family members, and friends. We were still in AIT (Advanced Individual Training) at this point. As an infantry soldier, we complete our basic training and AIT at the same location. They call it *One Station Unit Training* or OSUT. I miss my love Rachel and my family, but I did get to spend the weekend with them during family day so that was good. We went sightseeing in Columbus Georgia, ate some good food, and I was on cloud 9 after proposing to my soulmate. We didn't really have much alone time, but we'll make up for that on the honeymoon. I also have an extended family here with my battle buddies.

My close friends, Clifton Jones and now Julian Rodgers, are like my brothers here. We cut up all the time and stay getting smoked, but we do take our careers as soldiers seriously and ace all our tests. We set the standard when it comes to paper and practical exercises as well as our PT test, due to high scores and near perfect execution. We're always trying to outdo each other which helps us stay competitive and exceed our goals in OSUT. The tactical and combat training is great! I don't much care for the sleep deprivation part, but we train like we are in a live war time environment with live fire and combat training missions. We also do war games conducted without live ammo.

This allows us to practice tactical movements, scouting, surprise attacks, and capturing techniques. We are essentially the first line of defense for the rest of the military and clear the way to set up camp in what was known as enemy territory. I plan on going to ranger and airborne school at some point in my career. My heart condition has become more stable with exercise and occasional need for ACE inhibitor meds, so I should be good regarding training. When I said I wanted the full soldier experience, I meant it! But with Cliff being from the Southside of Chicago, and Julian (Rod as we call him) being from Upstate New York, our dynamic as a squad is pretty well-rounded. Cliff isn't a grunt like me or Julian. His MOS (Military Occupational Specialty) is a 19K or 19 kilo which is a Tanker. He drives tanks and blows stuff up, which is awesome! I'm a little jealous of him because of it. We're all expert marksman and can lead an entire company through precarious land nav situations. But we all sat or stood there wondering what our next course of action would be after 9/11. Would we be going to war as our 1st Sergeant suggested? Was it him just trying to hype us up? Either way, I was ready...

After weeks of rigorous training, mental and physical, we reached our **Turning Blue** ceremony which was our time to fully graduate OSUT. Once we graduated, I had a little time to spend with my loved ones before heading to my permanent duty station. We all got our orders by this time. Rod and I were both stationed at Fort Campbell Kentucky, while Cliff still had some time left before he completed his training. He would know his next duty assignment from there. We were both excited to be a part of history and one of the most prestigious divisions in the Army. *The 101st Airborne (Air Assault) Screaming Eagles!* With the attacks by foreign terrorist on American soil that occurred on 9/11, I knew my brothers and I would get deployed to fight sooner or later. Being a part of the 3rd brigade and *187th Airborne Infantry Regiment (Rakkasans)*, fighting for our country and freedom was inevitable.

It was later confirmed by the President that we would be going to war with the Taliban in Afghanistan and Saddam Hussein's regime in Iraq. I made sure Rachel and I got married before my unit deployed. Anything could happen in war, so I wanted to make sure we took that step and I set her up good financially in the event I didn't make it home... We found out Cliff was stationed in Fort Bliss Texas with the *1st Armored Division Combat Unit (Old Ironsides)*. He was actually my best man at our wedding. Rod was there as one of my groomsmen as well. I opted to wear my Class-A uniform opposed to a traditional tuxedo. My soon to be wife, Rachel, looked like an angel wearing an astonishing wedding dress that lit up the room. I couldn't help but cry tears of joy as my amazingly beautiful bride made her way down the aisle. Rachel's niece was the flower girl and nephew was the ring bearer. We exchanged vows and rings as Cliff whispered in my ear and teased about how corny my speech was. I smirked a bit as I shushed him and put the ring on her finger. Funny story about the ring... I gave her a ring pop at first as an engagement ring and told her not to get tempted to eat it. She then gave me "the finger;" and a lifesaver and said to make sure I don't lose any more weight, so it always fits. And if my ring finger gets too fat, to keep it in my wallet for good measure. We like to prank and joke each other like that. But from that day I told her I would buy the best ring that my little money could buy. She said she didn't care as long as I had her heart and she had mine. From there the search for a ring worthy of my queen was on. I used to work at a shipyard and did some photojournalism work before I enlisted into the Army. I've saved money since high school and my parents matched what I had. I was able to purchase her a stunning rock that I hoped she would love and cherish. I know it sounds crazy, but I heard the ring calling out to me... not like *Gollum* from *The Lord of The Rings,* but it was a little voice in my head and feeling in my gut that was urging me to buy it. Ok, maybe it was a little like *Gollum,* minus the part where he's obsessively ogling 'my precious' in the movie... But it wasn't at a big retailer either. It was a smaller franchise that I happened to discover while shopping one day. I appraised the ring and it was worth way more than I paid for it. Just more confirmation that we were destined to be together.

After we said I do, we jumped the broom, and I let out a loud **HOOAH,** as everyone applauded while we left the church. Once we made it to the reception, the DJ got everyone dancing with songs from Faith Hill and Janet Jackson. He also played classics like *The Cha Cha Slide,* and *Macarena* to name a few. I'm a terrible dancer, but we did have our slow dance and cake cutting ceremony. Cliff had jokes for me right away that night...

"Man, you can't dance to save your life! And though you're still ugly as sin, and have a deformed head, I'm proud of you for marrying such a lovely woman like Rachel. You know she's too good for you right?!" He said as Rod and I started cracking up.

"Yeah, I know I don't deserve her... I appreciate that bro! Means a lot coming from an overgrown *Chucky* doll." I said as we busted out laughing and had a small roast session.

"How about you Rod, any special ladies in your life?" Cliff

said with a glass a wine in his hand.

"Of course! You know women love me! Just kidding... I date on occasion but don't have a special someone yet. Just waiting for the right one you know."

"Well, don't wait too long, you know that saltpeter they gave us in training messes with our junk right? The longer you wait, the smaller it gets... don't do your balls like that man, It ain't worth it! But dude, we have some wild parties back in the barracks! I got so messed up one time, I didn't know what was going on. I woke up the next day on the floor in my draws. They said they got me on camera messing with some strippers they invited. Dollar bills, booty sweat, and empty bottles everywhere! You sure you want to be married?" Cliff said jokingly with his hand on my shoulders.

"Dude you're still a fool I see... and that saltpeter was BS!" I said as we all started laughing even louder.

"Of course! That's never gonna change! But on a serious note. I'm concerned about this war... I mean this is what we signed up for I guess... but I didn't think it would happen so soon... Hey Ricky, you think if we killed someone on deployment, we'll be damned to hell? You know the Bible says, 'thou shalt not kill' right?!"

"I don't think so... I don't have a heaven or hell to put anyone in, but I believe God would understand as we aren't doing it in cold blood. It would be for our protection and it's a part of our job. And we do a lot of bad things that God forgives if we repent and ask Him to Cliff. This would be no different I think... but like you said, we signed up for this and now have an opportunity to fight for what we believe in."

We all went to church while in OSUT. It was like our home away from home. I've never been super religious, but I always believed in God. My grandparents helped me with my understanding of church etiquette and the Bible as they attended faithfully. I broke down a few times when we went to service while in training and felt a sense of reconnection during that time. We had deep discussions because of it.

"I mean I get that, and I did sign up to serve our country, but are we really fighting for what we believe in? I know you're a real American hero Ricky that stands for truth; justice, and the American way and all, but is this really our war to fight in?" Rod said concerned as he jumped into the conversation.

"Well, even if it isn't our fight per say, the terrorists made it perfectly clear that they don't value our lives and we have to protect our people and our nation. Tearing down their regimes and hate organizations will help us do that." I said sternly.

Rachel walked up at that moment and gave me a look of endearment. I knew it was time to cut our conversation short and spend time with my bride.

"Hey boys! You mind if I take my husband for a spin on the dance floor real quick?"

"Yes ma'am! Please take this two left feet having clown with you." Cliff said as he chuckled and hit my arm.

"Please do! He's boring the mess out of us, " said Rod giving Cliff a pound.

"Hahaha, forget you guys!"

Laughing, Rachel grabbed my arm and pulled me to the danced floor. Though I have no rhythm, we danced the night away. It was just me and her in that moment. Timeless moments like these, tend to stay with you forever...

"Get down! We're taking enemy fire!" Yelled our Staff Sergeant as we took cover behind a nearby Humvee. "We need to lay down cover fire and flush them out!"

We were ambushed and taking indirect fire stationed miles outside of Kandahar in Afghanistan. The attack happened during the day on an operation to eliminate the Taliban threat, and reestablish the government in that area. It was only a few months after I was stationed at Fort Campbell before I was deployed on my first mission. I was a PFC (Private First Class) currently but was working on fast-tracking to E4 or Specialist rank. My adrenaline was pumping as I grabbed my M4 rifle and opened fire in the direction of the gunshots. I was on my first deployment after we declared war on the Taliban and Iraqi government. It certainly wouldn't be my last... but I made it out of my first few gunfights without being injured. I had multiple confirmed kills by this time as well. The blood and gore from the bodies we hit or bombed, can definitely haunt your dreams... The question that Cliff asked me at my wedding reception played in my head every time I pulled the trigger. Still, I didn't hesitate to do so as it could cost lives if we took too long to engage. Though it was challenging as some of the targets could be smaller than the weapons they carried... we did what we had to do to survive... It did seem like I had a guardian angel watching over me out there as I had several close calls where bullets flew right by me...

By this time, I completed the necessary training to get promoted to Sergeant as well as completed Army airborne, air assault, and ranger school. Rod and I were proud to be a part of the *75th Ranger Regiment Unit*. An elite group of brave soldiers who were lean, mean, fighting machines, able to take someone out with their bare hands! The hand to hand combat training was awesome! I'll eventually have to register my hands as lethal weapons because of it. Just kidding, that's the combat training still talking. But Rachel and I had a son now, which was great! I've always wanted a son! Someone who could follow in my footsteps and keep the Myers legacy alive. We have been going through a rough patch in our marriage though, which is due mainly to my deployments. She wants me to get out of the Army because I'm always gone, and she fears for my life. I understand where she's coming from, but I love what I do. Ok, maybe not the long deployments or being away from my family but being a soldier; It's given me purpose, and I'm thankful for that. I enlisted for 4 years initially but have moved up in the ranks fairly quickly. With all of the marital issues we've been having, I don't think I should reenlist, though I think about it often. Rachel has been patient with me and has done her best to put up with me being deployed. My rough transition back to garrison and home life after deployment is also concerning. It's hard to shut it off when being a soldier 24/7 has been engrained in you. We are scheduled to deploy any moment to fight in **the second Gulf War**. I have a unit that I'm responsible for and have to lead them into battle. Rod is in my unit now and one of my troops. It's a little weird to have him as a subordinate, but I don't let that get in the way of our friendship. Even though it's fun to pull rank on him every now and again.

"Hey Sarge, how are things with you and the Mrs.?" Rod said as he was loading gear on one of our tactical vehicles.

"Not doing to good Specialist Rodgers. She took my son and went to stay with her parents for a while. She said she still loves me but wants the man she first fell in love with. I don't know what to do Rod, Rachel and my son mean everything to me. More than these stripes and this uniform." I said starting to tear up.

"Man, I hate hearing that Sarge. Being an Army wife is no easy task especially when their husband deploys every 6 months it seems like. Plus, you have a lumpy mashed potato head, so I know it's even harder to deal with." He said as I cracked a smile.

"I thought Cliff was the only one that was supposed to give me grief."

"Just trying to fill his shoes until he gets back. You know I can be a jerk when I want to be. Speaking of Cliff, when's the last time you spoke with him?"

"It's been a minute... and don't remind me. We were about to fight that one time you set me up. I promise I wanted to beat the life out of you with a bar of soap. But last I heard his unit was being deployed to Iraq as well. He also got promoted to Sergeant. Time for you to catch up! What's the holdup Specialist?!" I said in a joking yet serious tone.

"I don't know Sarge, nerves I guess. Just haven't fully bought into the dream like you have, you know. And I remember that. That was hilarious! Yeah, I had something to prove in OSUT. Had to show everyone that I wasn't a push over. Alpha dog mentality. I still can't believe you almost died trying to motivate me to keep going though. You were nuts!"

"Yeah that was pretty crazy huh? I'd do it again too! Even though you were and forever will be a winey douchebag... and my aortic stenosis is more under control now, so I've been ok. Though I've suffered from panic attacks and night terrors recently." I said while wiping my sweaty palms on my legs.

"I bet! War would do that to anyone; and now, I'll get my share of it, hooah..." he said sarcastically.

June, 2003

As rangers in the 75th regiment, it was our duty to infiltrate hostile enemy territory and clear the way for the rest of the military to advance. We were great at what we did. Quick, precise, and deadly when we needed to be. We had *M1 A2 Abrams* tanks and *Black Hawk* helicopters that supported us during our missions in Iraq. We made our way through Baghdad and Mosul where we had intel on multiple terrorists who were seeking solace and protection there. We had numerous casualties in our search for **weapons of mass destruction** and our war on terrorism. Thankfully, we haven't had any deaths in my squad as of yet... I prided myself on that, but mainly my troops for being a solid unit that watched our six. I was always angered when we heard about our soldiers being brutally killed. I had a terrible sinking feeling in my stomach that our luck would eventually run out...

One day, we were doing our normal routine where we took a couple of units and convoyed through the crowded cities of Iraq, looking for supplies, and scouting the area for potential threats. I had a four-man crew riding with me. One of my troops carried an M203 grenade launcher (one of my favorite weapons in war). We usually have armored vehicles with a mounted 50-caliber turret, and a gunner who had an M249 light machine gun (SAW as we called it) travel with us on missions. We only had a gunner on this trip which was our lead vehicle. We usually station them throughout the convoy in the front, middle or rear as we traveled. We did this intentionally to give us more coverage in case of an ambush. Suddenly, there was a loud explosion. The lead vehicle just got hit with an IED (Improvised Explosive Device) and we were ambushed from all sides.

"Sarge! I'm hit I'm hit!" Yelled one of my troops.

"Man down!" Screamed another.

Anytime we were in the thick of a fire fight, my adrenaline would shoot through the roof, but I was still poised and knew what to do. This attack was different...

"We need to set up a perimeter!" I shouted as I dropped and low crawled to the back of the vehicle.

"But Sarge, they are shooting from every angle and could have RPG's" (Rocket Propelled Grenades), said Rod as he was down on the ground next to me.

"Ok, we have to make our way to shelter first. We have men down and no way to get to them. We have to keep laying down cover fire while I radio in for help!" I hollered at Rod and my troops who were sprawled on the ground returning fire.

We had a radio in the vehicle behind the one hit by the IED. It was in front of the vehicle we were in. I had to make a run for it and risk exposing myself to gunfire. As I made my way to the front of our vehicle, I looked out of the corner of my eye and saw a young boy with a bomb strapped to his chest... I froze in that moment as I thought about my own son and what I would do if I saw him like that. After I shook it off, I yelled "bomber 3 o clock!" As I aimed and got ready to pull the trigger, I felt heat in my legs, side, and shoulder. I was hit! I didn't let that take my focus off of the bomber. But suddenly, he dropped to the ground and I saw Rod running towards him. He jumped on him right as the bomb exploded and saved our lives. Wounded, I managed to radio for help in what seemed like an eternity of fighting for our lives. Thankfully, a nearby unit was already in route as they heard the reverb of gunshots ringing out as the menacing battle continued. I lost several good men that day... all valuable... but losing Rod hurt the most...

I was shot multiple times and lost a lot of blood during the fight. I had several surgeries and was in and out of consciousness, so I don't remember much. However, I do remember having several out of body experiences... I saw myself on the hospital bed as well as had visions of me killing corrupt people for money... Freaked me out really... But once I was sent home, Rachel was there by my side every step of my recovery. We are expecting another child and are closer than we've ever been since I came back from the war. I've also visited Cliff since I've been back in garrison. He lost both of his legs in a mortar attack that hit one of his vehicles while they were away from their tanks. Even in a wheelchair, he's in good spirits and jokes about being a human tank now. Me on the other hand, am angry all the time due to the countless loss of life and what I experienced during this deployment. I could have been killed and never got a chance to say goodbye, like so many soldiers who died over there. Never having the opportunity to say **goodbye** or **see you later** to loved ones, scares me til this day. Though I received a bronze star and purple heart, I feel like I don't deserve it...

I lost great people that day. Soldiers. Brothers. Warriors. I'm no hero... Rod was the real hero and his brave actions saved our lives. I told them I didn't want to take it but wanted them to make sure **Specialist Julian Rodgers** was honored and remembered for giving his life that day. War is never easy or a pretty sight... The onslaught of terror continued with thousands of soldiers dying or injured during these wars. Some who were mutilated, beheaded, and had their naked bodies paraded in the streets like trophy kills... Others executed and burned alive. The horrors of war, death, and destruction seemed insurmountable. Was it really worth it? The bureaucracy of it all? Are we really free or is it just a mirage? Institutionalism under the guise of democracy? Or propaganda perpetuated by political gain and media persuasion? I asked myself those questions until the terrorists of 9/11 were brought to justice and soldiers were brought home from Afghanistan and Iraq. I still ask myself those questions as I deal with PTSD, panic attacks, and night terrors that will haunt me for the rest of my life...

16

As the plot unfolds the bullets reload.
It's automatic; turning victims' brain
Fragments to magnets the outcome
Is tragic traumatic crack magic
Got addicts acrobatic erratic.
Athletes of the streets, who score rocks
And elude the police the hunger for sweets
The triple 6 beast who laughs when they feast, and Families get grief.
How easily the living becomes deceased.
A motif is created to remember the person behind the pain. The name behind the stain,
And the rain that hits the pane.
Left on a broken heart, too soon to depart.
From a world that barely knew them.
A world that would spew them out of its mouth even if they were hot or cold no doubt about it.
But I'm thankful for the ones who paved and gave their lives so we could be free.
I'm not going to throw away my opportunity to fulfill my destiny my battle; is continuous light through the continual abyss, we exist to coexist not to risk eternal bliss.
We fall sometimes we slip, but never lose your grip on your reality.
Let black history be more than just a memory, the shortest month doesn't hinder me.

I hear the negro spirituals quietly, can't silence me.
I hear my ancestors calling repeatedly, we sing.
Lift every voice, let it ring.
Your greatness, let it sting. **Finnis--**

As I finished reading my black history month poem out loud to the class, I was waiting for a slow clap or a "yo that was dope" from some of my classmates. But all I was met with was a "not bad L, but I would like to see you after class to discuss it further," my African American studies teacher Mrs. Frye said vehemently. This was my last class of the day. I like the class, but she is always on my case about something. I can't catch a break... As the bell rang and everyone left, Mrs. Frye called me to her desk.

"Hey L, you mind telling me what was up with your poem today?"

"What do you mean Mrs. Frye? It came from the heart and a real place. It had a positive ending, but I write about what I know and what I've experienced. Drugs, violence, poverty, it's where I come from." I said slightly irritated.

"You come from Kansas last I checked. That is a state, and you may have experienced those things, but that does not have to define who you are or how you live your life. I think you are a very talented writer and would love for you to recite this in front of the school for our *Black History Month Presentation.* I just want you to rewrite some of the rough parts and really dig deep to express what this month, and black history in general, means to you. I want your perspective as a young black man but want to hear how you will become the change you want to see in the world." She said as she handed back my poem.

"Yes ma'am, I will do my best to come up with something that you old folks could appreciate," I said as we both shared a laugh before I left.

I pride myself on having an extensive vocabulary as I used to study the dictionary to help me become a better writer or word-smith. I want to be able to conversate with anyone about business. Which I plan on being a millionaire someday. My name is Larry, but I go by L. It was kind of my rap name. I wanted to use the name *Logic,* but it was already taken by a dope MC. Then I wanted to go by *LL*, but that name was taken by one of the legends in hip-hop as well. So, I just go by L now, and when people ask me what it stands for, I say it stands for Lyrical, not Larry... They then say it should stand for lame because that's what you are and we start laughing or fighting from that point. But I'm kind of a big deal, well at least I was before I moved to Washington D.C. It's not bad here, and I've dealt with worse in terms of crime and violence when I was living out in the Midwest. But being the new kid wasn't easy... I just transferred to D.C. after living in Kansas for a while. I was getting into trouble with gangs, drugs, and stealing so my parents thought it would be best that I spent some time living with my grandparents to change the scenery.

I also got shot at several times. One of which was during a rap battle, but they don't know about that. They would flip out if they knew their 16-year-old son was in the streets like that. I'm fortunate to not catch a case for the stuff I did out there. I did spend my 9th grade and most of my 10th grade year suspended or in detention for fighting and cutting class, so I'm trying to make my last couple of years in high school count. Though I miss my real homies and my folks back home, I think this is the new start I need to get my life back on track. My grandparents are in the church heavy and I believe in God and all, just don't feel like I have to be in church 7 days a week... ok, maybe I'm exaggerating a little, but it sure does seem like we're always there...

"Larry, how's it going baby?"

"Hey grandma! Going good... How are you and Pop Pop

doing?"

"We're doing well, just getting things ready for dinner."

"Smells good! What are we having?!" I said as my stomach was touching my back.

"Fried chicken, collard greens, fried okra, mac n' cheese and cornbread. Also, sweet potato pie for dessert." She said as she was washing the greens and preparing the pot of water.

Granny always made those meals that give you the itis right afterwards. Everyday seemed like Thanksgiving or a Sunday meal at her house. I love it when we get those bushels of crabs too. They're messy, but worth it. I been here since last summer so a few months now. I haven't made many friends as I have a hard time trusting people. I keep my circle small and grass cut low to watch out for snakes. I do have a couple of dudes I hang out with though. I met them at lunch one day. They were having a rap battle in the cafeteria and I roasted the dude that was supposed to be legit. Everybody freaked out and started cheering. My video got thousands of views online too. They even remixed the part when I said:

Call me the King like *T'Challa,* your teeth look like *Baraka,* finish him like *Mortal Kombat* rip your arms off call me Jax, better yet call me smack, you're too wack to battle rap, kill any MC on wax, no continues no coming back, facts." I said a lot of other random stuff too, but that's the part people talked about the most for some reason... When you battle, you pretty much say whatever messed up thing that comes to mind to roast the other person.

The punchlines have to make sense for it to be dope as well. I have way better bars than that, but I got the W so it's cool. Though 'freestylin' is fun, I'd rather write my raps so I can think about my delivery and what I want to say more in depth. I've been to the studio on numerous occasions and recorded several demos. I was even starting to buzz a little bit before I moved. I plan on working on a mixtape at some point. But I'm an old soul so I like *Nas*, *DMX*, *Jay-Z*, *Biggie*, *Pac*, *Snoop*, *Dr. Dre,* and *Bone Thugs N Harmony* to name a few. Those are the MCs that have influenced me the most. But that day made me feel like I was back home in Kansas as I was the man at my old school. My ability to rap and charismatic nature, got me the money, girls, and respect from my peers. I was going places; until I was set up by one of my "homeboys" and got jumped by a rival gang. They messed me up pretty bad to where I had to get staples in my head and pins in my legs. That's the main reason my folks sent me to live with my grandparents. They are well cultured so maybe they could teach me more about our heritage and the importance of carrying ourselves respectfully as black men and women. I still see it as I'm young and have my whole life ahead of me, so I'm allowed to make mistakes or bad choices every now and again... Nobody's perfect, but I do want to make my family proud and leave a positive impact on this world. In the meantime, I'll try to convince my granny to let me go to this party tonight. I can't lie to her, but I don't have to tell her all of the details either.

"Hey granny, me and some of my friends are having a get together tonight. Would it be cool if I go hang out for a minute?"

"I don't know Larry, are their parents going to be there?" She said as she pulled her glasses down to look at me closer.

"I'm not sure granny, but I'll be responsible." I said in hopes of convincing her to let me go.

"You're not sexually active are you? I don't want to hear from the OAG (Office of Attorney General) talking about you owe child support or something... cause if you're man enough to play, you're man enough to pay..."

"Granny! Man, you get straight to the point huh?! And I do use protection. But we are just trying to chill and maybe play some games."

"Ok, as long as you are careful and not getting caught up.

These girls will have your nose wide open... I just want you to make good decisions and think about your future, that's all. I know you will make mistakes as we all do, but if I can help guide you in the right direction, that's what I'm going to do." She said sincerely.

"I appreciate that and love you for it granny. I'll be fine though. I've been raised by amazing parents and grandparents." I said hoping to butter her up some.

"Yeah yeah yeah, I hear you." She said not fallen for my adulation.

"I may need your help rewriting my black history month poem that I was asked to recite in front of the whole school. My teacher Mrs. Frye is always on my case no matter how hard I work..."

"It's probably because she sees something in you that we all see, your greatness. And with greatness comes sacrifice and pressure. You can't make a diamond without pressure. I'll take a look at it while you head out. I want you back by eleven o clock sharp, you hear me?"

"Yes ma'am, will do!" I said geeked because she said yes.

Chuck's or **Jordan's** was the way to go out west, so I think I'll follow suit here. This was my first time hanging out with my boys since I moved so it should be fun. I don't have anything to prove so a white tee and khaki's it is.

"You sure you don't want to stay home and work on this poem with me?"

"I'm good granny, I'll work on it when I come back. Appreciate your help with it though!" I said as I made my way out the door.

Now every crew has to have a crazy white boy or crazy Hispanic dude in it to be legit. I'm lucky enough to be cool with a white and Hispanic dude in my squad. Well he's mixed but it still counts. His name is Matt Keller, but we call him Kellz. Not to be confused with *MGK.* And then I have my Asian homie Kenneth G Lin, but we call him Kenny G. Not to be confused with... well you know who I'm talking about... but this was the squad. They know what I was into back in Kansas so they looked at me like the cool black guy that they should learn everything from. They humored me a lot because of it. But Matt was wearing holey jeans and a holey shirt. He was definitely a rebel and got into trouble a lot because of it. He had easy access to drugs and alcohol as his folks had money. He also got an all-black BMW 3 series whip for his 16th birthday, so people think he's spoiled. Which he is, but he'll also look out for you if you need something. Kenny was more of a laid-back skater type. He was a loaner but liked to joke a lot and was a class clown. He's a hip-hop head and has a library of vinyl that would put any record shop to shame. Yes vinyl is still a thing... They both keep me rolling and cutting up in school. We mesh well together. My crew!

"Dude this party's bout to be off da chain! There are going to be a lot of hot girls at this party no lie! I heard Nani Miller and her cheerleading crew are going to be there! Dude you should rap like *Eminem* in the movie *8 mile* and choke on purpose. Then come back and kill it like he did!" Matt said as he lit up a blunt.

"Nah, I'm good on that. Just there to chill and hangout. Although, if they have an open mic and a **WACK** MC that needs to be scorched, I may have to do somethin about it..."

"That's what I'm talking about! My man!" He said as he coughed from inhaling the blunt smoke too long.

Now I don't really smoke anymore, I'll have an occasional drink though, but I get too paranoid when I smoke. I also like to have a level head when I'm in strange surroundings. I especially want to be in my right mind when I talk to Nani. She was perfect. Hazel brown eyes, honey glazed skin, immaculate complexion, and a brilliant mind. Everything I wanted in a woman. I've never been the shy type, so I did shoot my shot a couple times. But she's messin with some football jock named Derek, so I backed off. I played football too and ran track. So I got some burners on me when I need to make moves. Well, I did have burners before I got jumped and got pins in my legs... But being the new kid, I'm still trying to find my way. She seems to give off mixed messages though. We talk all the time in our African American studies class as well as Civics. Ok so maybe I flirt with her and she just laughs, but she did hold my hand one time and said she loved my poems so that was cool.

"Hey L, we've known you for a few months now. Is it cool to say the *N-word* around you?" Kenny said as him and Matt looked at me with intrigue.

"Absolutely not! It's never ok for you to say the *N-word,* you're not black!" I said as I shook my head in disbelief.

"But all the rappers say it, and you say it to other black people. So why can't we?"

"I mean you both are minorities so it may be a little easier to accept coming from you, but my thing is, why don't we call each other kings or queens instead of a word that has a negative connotation to it. I mean I do use the word sometimes, but when I use it, I'm sayin we're **Never Ignorant Getting Goals Accomplished** or **Now I'm Going to Get Above it All**."

"Dope!" Matt and Kenny said in unison.

"See that's why we mess with you bro, you're always dropping knowledge on us!" Matt said as he dapped me up.

"Yeah that's why we mess with you." Kenny said as he tried to pass me the blunt.

They didn't even realize I got that saying from a remixed Pac song. That's why I loved these dudes, anything excites them. And they welcomed me to the school when no one else did. I consider them my day one homies...

"Nah I'm good man, maybe later... I'm trying to keep my head in the game for tonight. How much longer do we have anyway?" I said with my palms sweaty anxious to get to the party.

"Man we still have about 30 minutes to go." Matt said thumbing the steering wheel.

"30 minutes! We've been driving for an hour it seems like. Just make sure you're going the speed limit; we can't afford to get pulled over and be even more late to the party."

"Relax L, I got this my G. Just sit back and let me drive. And you're right, we definitely don't want to get pulled over. Check in the glove box."

"What's this! What are you doing with a Glock 45 in your glove box Kellz?!"

"It's for protection. You know I'm pushing weight now. Trying to be in your league big dawg."

"Nah bro, this isn't what you need to be doing now. I lived that life, had a similar piece, but realized that ain't the life you really want to live."

"Don't get all lame on me now L, you're the OG, we look up to you. Go ahead. Pick it up. Don't forget where you came from too much."

I picked up the gun Kellz had in his glove box and felt like

Pac in juice. You do get a sense of power when you hold a weapon. As I pointed it at the dashboard, I saw red and blue flashing lights behind us.

"Dude, it's the cops!" Kenny yelled, as we all started to freak out a little.

"Ok, just be calm and let me handle this. My dad's a lawyer so I know our rights. I forgot to tell y'all, I have drugs in the middle console. I'm not talking about weed, but the hard stuff." Matt said looking at us with worry in his eyes.

"I've dealt with the cops on several occasions, they're not all bad. But the ones that are, usually don't like people of color. We just have to do what they say, and we'll get through this." I said trying to keep a level head.

"But you're black dude! You know how racist cops can be towards you and your people." Kenny said trying to empathize with me.

"I know bro, but we have to play it cool."

As the officer approached, my stomach was in a knot. The car had to have smelled like weed and there was an illegal pistol in the glovebox, and drugs in the center console. We still have to play it cool if we want to make it through this...

"Good evening, do you know why I pulled you over?"

"No officer, why is that?" Matt said with a little attitude.

"You were swerving back there. License and registration please. Have you had anything to drink tonight?"

There were two police officers. One on Kellz side and one on mine. I made sure I had my hands on the dash where they could see them and didn't make any sudden moves.

"No sir, I'm as clean as a whistle."

"I'm going to need everyone to step out of the car please." The officer said with a stern tone.

"But sir, what did we do wrong?! I'm not given you permission to search my car for anything. I know my rights; you can't search my vehicle unless I consent!"

"Shut your mouth! I didn't say we were going to search your car yet, but since you want to be smart about it, we're going to search every inch of your vehicle. Out of the car now! I won't tell you again!"

Now I've been in cuffs and ruffed up by the police before but came out alive each time. Nowadays you'll get shot by police for not complying or responding to simple commands.

"Chill Kellz! Just get out of the car." I said trying to plead with him.

"No! They don't have the right to take us out of the car and search the vehicle!" He yelled back.

I'm sure the cops smelled the weed smoke in the car, even though we rolled the windows down to air it out a while ago. This would give them probable cause to search the vehicle. But Kellz is on one because we're hot. There are drugs and an unregistered firearm in the car. We're all looking at possible jail time for this... As the cop pulled Kellz out of the driver seat, the other cop grabbed me and threw me to the ground. Kenny slowly got out of the car, got on the ground and put his hands behind his head. At that moment Kellz screams, "grab the gun!" One of the officers yelled "he has a gun!" Shots rang out and I ran! I don't know why I ran, but I ran until I couldn't run anymore. I knew I didn't want to be another victim of police brutality. I hope everyone is ok. I know I just fled the scene and the cops will probably come looking for me. At least if they get me while I'm at home, I have a better chance of coming out of it alive... I can't let my grandparents know what happened until the morning. I'll just go home, play it cool, and use this as motivation to write my poem. It may be the last poem I write for a while as a free man.

As I made it home, my grandma was asleep on the couch. She made edits to my poem and left me some food in the fridge. She is an awesome woman. I hate that I let her down like this... I knew Kellz was crazy, but I didn't see this coming. We didn't even make it to the party... I received text messages from Nani asking where I was too... another opportunity for something good to happen in my life that I missed out on... I still can have a rap career if this all blows over. Plenty of successful rappers out there who caught a case, did time, and made a positive impact in the world when they bounced back. Speaking of rap career, let me finish my poem for this black history month presentation.

I'm free, I'm free, from the bonds that shackled me.
Yes free from my oppressors.
Free from second guessers. Free from self-hate, free from a reprobate mind, will it stand the test of time.
Only time will tell.
The emancipation proclamation was a great start to Abolish slavery; Juneteenth, the 13th Amendment we Are truly free; but sometimes it doesn't look that way To me; when we still see hate crimes and countless unarmed black people killed on TV.
Police brutality criminality can't you see?
Society turns a blind eye and needs optometry.
We can't wait to unify, for now is the time.
Wake up the blind make no mistake.
Negative seeds of hate penetrate deep into the soul and don't escape.
White man white man, why do you fear what you don't understand.
Black man black man, why do we kill our own I don't understand.

Is it proximity, is it jealousy?
We're all created equally so why idolatry it bothers me that we can be so easily distracted by the enemy.
Which can be the inner me or lack of synergy; nonetheless we're still blessed to have examples set before us, Yes blessed:
Frederick Douglass, Harriet Tubman, Dr. King, Malcolm X, Who's next?
Is it you? Is it me?
Let's put our differences to the side and change humanity.
Yes we're free, yes we're free, from the bonds that shackled thee.
Free to be great, as the time will no longer wait.
Free to speak free to live. Free to love free to give.
The change it starts with us, when in God will we trust. **Finnis**--

As Mrs. Frye recited my poem to the school, some cheered, and some cried. You see, I didn't make it out alive that night. The cops shot me and Kellz several times and killed us. Kenny survived as he stayed on the ground while they were shooting. The strange thing is, they never found the gun in the glovebox... My funeral was packed and full of friends and loved ones from all over. Even people I didn't expect to be there like Nani and a few homeboys from back home showed up for the service. I'm thankful I got a chance to make a difference in people's lives that day. That poem meant a lot to me, especially after my grandma recited it again during my funeral. It broke my heart to see her and my family in tears. I hope they can forgive me and that they are proud of the poem and memories I left behind. The poem that inspired me to want to change my life for the better. I hope it encourages those that hear it to live free and do their best to be great at what they love to do. Remember life is but a vapor, the morning dew won't last, 40 acres and a mule we're owed, we'll pursue til our time has passed. **Finnis—**

KILL SWITCH

The year is 2042, and I know what you're thinking; there are fly-ing cars, cyborgs, and laser weapons that can level an entire city with one irreparable blast. Though we've made profound leaps in technological advancements, our society now is more like the movie *Mad Max* or *Turbo Kid*, than *Total Recall* or *The Fifth Elem-ent.* This in part is due to the second civil war that divided our country indefinitely... Racial discrimination and social injustice has been prevalent in our world since the beginning of time. From slavery to the holocaust; from the civil rights movement to the murder of George Floyd and Breonna Taylor and countless others who have been victims of police brutality. History has a way of repeating itself... But our country and world have been spiraling out of control for a while and has literally fallen off its axis. The virus killed over one-fourth of the world's population. Global warming and extreme weather events took a few million as well. Now the world is segregated into 4 divisions or factions based on the earth's hemispheres. Though the world is a massive place, the prime meridian and equator gave us an idea of how the factions would be divided. The Northern, Southern, Eastern or Western hemisphere is what we migrated too based on what we believed in. The powers that be thought this would help with bringing solidarity back to our way of life. But how can you bring harmony when dystopia is what we've become accustomed to?

This was a global effort though, but there were a lot of casual-ties along the way... Nuclear warfare almost destroyed the entire world, but the *UN* was able to come to a compromise and legis-lation went into effect to determine how countries or societies would be governed going forward. This was after much bloodshed in the second civil war. No side won really, but a cease fire was called to try to preserve life and salvage our tattered society and broken judicial system. They used the Greek alphabet to label our factions based on the region and our political or societal preferences. I guess that was the most efficient way to go about it in their eyes. Plus, they wanted to thwart any sedition that would come there way because of it. But, Alpha, Beta, Gamma, and Delta region is how we are identified now. Sorry Omegas, they didn't take it that far... If you were in the Northern hemisphere you were an Alpha, Southern Deltas, Eastern Betas, and Western Gammas. We have 16 states in the southern region, each with their own base and leadership structure. I heard we even have allies in South America and Africa which I thought was cool. The Alphas considered themselves to be among the elite and alt-right in their beliefs. Beta was a close second to that. Gammas had rebels but were opportunists at best. And then you have the Deltas.

Us common folks who don't want anyone to tell us how to live our lives. The government let us choose which faction we wanted to belong to based on a consensus; however, we Deltas are treated like second rate citizens as we do not conform to the status quo. So we basically had to fight or barter for years to solidify everything we have and everything we've built for our faction to sustain itself. We do what we have to do to survive and don't play nice with outsiders. We've learned our lesson from that and choose to protect our own. We have NO TRESPASSING signs set up all around our campsite. We also have PROCEED WITH CAUTION signs posted close to our operations and military base. It's the way it has to be now to prevent sabotage or the infiltration of other factions who may want to take over our land and resources or proselyte our people... We've heard other factions have actual severed heads on spikes to ward off intruders. I'm sure that's very effective but we didn't take it that far... I know I wouldn't want to take a wrong turn and end up in their territory... but the government did allow us to vote on who we wanted in office and to represent our faction; like a senate, mayor or governor, so that was good. Whether you were Democrat, Republican, Socialist or Capitalist in your beliefs, we all could choose what group we wanted to support. But yep, that's who I represent and who I plan to advance in this crazy new society politics, anarchists, and lobbyists created.

Racial tension and political division came to a head in 2020. The height of the *Black Lives Matter* movement reached their pinnacle of support globally during this time. This was a good thing as the world became more unified at one point because of it. However, it showed the world how divided our nation really was regarding race and political belief systems. Blatant racism, hate crimes, and violent protests raged during this time. Militias and military forces were deployed on US soil against the American people to help regain order which only added fuel to the fire. Protesters labeled as *Antifa* or terrorist by their staunch right-wing counterparts, clashed for a few years until it all imploded and chaos ensued. It started with protests and riots across the nation. Then people started to exercise our Second Amendment right to bear arms more liberally. The problem with that was people began to take the law into their own hands and became vigilantes. Shooting people daily was the norm for them. People exercising our First Amendment rights, but also ones who threatened businesses or destroyed property were the main targets of the vigilantes. Even after the cease fire and end of the second civil war, violence was prevalent among factions. Each faction had their own line of defense with troops or soldiers that carried the heavy artillery. We all still carry some form of weapon to defend ourselves when we go on missions, men, women, and children alike. They tried to gentrify our communities to look more affluent as a society, but wanted to control how we lived our lives, so we became more defiant. We choose to live how we want in these archaic times, and only follow the laws of the land that help sustain our faction.

And I'm one hundred percent against things like police brutality, racial inequality, and social injustice; however, meeting violence with violence only begets more violence, and ultimately more carnage as a result. Which is why I was a pacifist until I was forced to fight and defend my family from vigilantes who shoot first, but don't ask questions later. The police were dismantled, government in disarray, and soon it seemed like it was every faction or family for themselves. Then in 2025, the powers that be came up with the **brilliant** idea to create a universal currency and chip that would help bring structure and some normalcy back to our nation and world. At least that's what they were advertising it would do... The technology has been in development since the late 90s and early 2000s, but the government found a way to make it work more extensively. A chip that has all of our vital information stored on it: Name, address, social security number, birth certificate, color, beliefs, banking info, all accessed by a wave of the hand (left or right depending upon your preference). We do our best to farm and ration our food, water, and supplies so we do not have to get the chip implant. However, we do have scouts and soldiers who have cut the chip out of someone's hand and used it to buy supplies. They tape it to their palm so when it's scanned, it will function as normal. I know it sounds barbaric, but try going weeks without toiletries, food, and water, and see if your mindset doesn't change... Let me ask you a question, do you believe in time travel? I do, and the craziest thing is I have proof! I was a photojournalist before everything went to hell in a hand-basket. I was freelance but worked with a lot of wealthy individuals and corporations. I'm also a history buff.

Throughout time, important people that have been pivotal in shaping the fabric of America's infrastructure, economy, work-force, and moral compass have been assassinated due to their ability to influence the multitudes. My faction and I believe there is a secret organization working with the government to use those who have influence for their own personal agendas. There have been different allegations of people showing up in past photos who are still in our present time. When you blow up certain images or iconic photos like Dr. Martin Luther King Jr.

greeting the people after winning the *Nobel Peace Prize,* or President John F. Kennedy before he was assassinated, you can see blurry shadowy figures that look like people in trench coats or hoodies. We believe they had something to do with monitoring and advancing the progress of public figures in our nation. Then, and in our present time... We also believe when these important figures served their purpose, the organization working with the government uses a chip to control, manipulate, and kill their subordinates. They make it look like the host died of natural causes like a heart attack or brain aneurism. The **Kill Switch** is what it's called among factions, but the government calls it the *Omnis* or *Everything Chip.* The multi-purpose electronic storage device was used for banking, barter, and basically everything needed to function in a normal society. They wanted to make it mandatory or law for every faction member to get the implant. We rebelled of course... This was the *coup de grâce* which caused us to lose hope in having a 'normal' society again...

The religious zealots call it the mark of the beast or the sign of the times. You know, the end of the world, Armageddon. Though it's not a triple 6 on your forehead or right hand as they suggest it would be, it has similar implications as the vision described in the Book of *Revelation* from the Bible. A vision that God gave one of his disciples about events that would cause the end of the Earth as we know it. It would then pave the way for a new heaven and earth for those who are believers. Some theologians attribute the writings of the Book of Revelation to John the apostle, while others say it was John of the island of Patmos in Greece just west of Turkey who wrote the book. All I know is, whoever wrote it, definitely seen some trippy stuff... Since Sunday school, I was always intrigued by the Bible, the story of Christ, and the **Book of Revelation.** And if my memory serves me correctly, that particular book, is nothing to play around with... But you may be wondering what all of this has to do with time travel. You see, the shadowy figures in trench coats and dark hoodies aren't from that time frame as the chip was fully developed and mass-produced in

2027. This secret organization found a way to create a chip and time travel to test it and change the events of history that may or may not have happened otherwise.

My faction has traced them back to Abraham Lincoln and his assassination. With the technology we have now, we're able to make images in pictures clearer when we expand them. This allows us to capture any excess energy or images the camera naturally picked up in the photo. You see, the hoodies were not from that time period. Though trench coats were a thing in the 1850s, Hoodies were manufactured in the 1930s and this sleeveless hoody the individual wore, was designed in modern times. We believe it's a woman based on the shape of the figure and the stories we've heard about *La Dama de la Muerte* or "The Lady of Death" during these times. She's not to be confused with *Santa Muerte* but any time you see her figure in a photo, the main figurehead in the photo ends up dead... I know this sounds like a stretch, but what if John Wilkes Booth was being controlled by the *Omnis-Chip* when he assassinated President Lincoln?

This can be viewed as a conspiracy theory, but we've hacked into the chip before and found programs uploaded to them that dealt with mood manipulation, and enhanced neuro capabilities. A chip this secret organization and the government could use to potentially make and control super soldiers. Imagine how much money they could make selling something invaluable like that. They've already made billions manufacturing the chip worldwide. But **Soldiers of fortune,** who could eradicate the enemy, and be dispose of with just the push of a button... The quintessential bad guys win again... unless we expose what they are really doing behind the scenes. Though I'm not a fighter per say, I'm resourceful and know how to take care of myself in this new age of gladiators and argonauts. Or better yet *Novus Ordo Seclorum,* **"New Order of The Ages."** I have been tasked with finding the woman in the photos we have of Abraham Lincoln and other historical figures. I am currently in Texas where Captain Ryan Johnson is in command. I've traced her carbon footprint to a base in the woods just east of here.

"Captain Johnson, how are you doing sir?"

"Doing good soldier, how are you?"

"I'm not a soldier sir, just a concerned citizen of Delta trying to improve our way of life here."

"Yeah, we definitely could use some improvements." He chuckled. "We have enough food, shelter and resources, but could use more footing in diplomacy and our economy as well. Also getting access to the **Kill Switch** and time travel capabilities, would help further advance our society."

"But sir, do we really need to time travel?" I said with a perplexed look on my face.

"Well, just think about what we could do and what we could change if we had the capability. The options are endless! We would be able to stop injustices and prevent calamities before they happened. We would be able to fight fire with fire and that's why I need you to find 'The Lady of Death' and try to convince her to help us. She is the source of this somehow." He said pinpointing coordinates on a map.

"I'll do my best sir..."

"That's all I ask... you are one of my best trackers, and I need you to take a few of our fighters and head west through the forest. We are picking up spikes in geothermal energy and barometric pressure out there. Could be her..."

"Yes sir, will do..."

Anytime there was time travel suspected in a region or area, the barometric pressure and geothermal temperature spiked. At least that's what our scientists and bio hackers tell us. I don't know what to say if it's her; after all, she is known as "The Lady of Death." Hopefully, the soldiers I take with me don't scare her off or cause her to butcher us all... We have gnarly vehicles with weaponry like the game *Twisted Metal* on *PlayStation.* We also travel by riding horses who are armored like they were in Medieval or Renaissance times. We chose to use military grade vehicles for our journey until we had to travel on foot. As we began our excursion through the pernicious forest, we were met with thick foliage, intense humidity, and disconcerting animal noises that made us all jumpy. I'm glad I brought the troops with me; They were armed to the teeth. I'm a good shot, but not that good under duress.

"Hey, did you hear something? I thought I heard a rustling in the bushes over there." Said Evans, one of the soldiers from our tactical team. "Yeah, I definitely heard something... I'm going to check it..." he said as he yelped before finishing his sentence.

"Evans?! You good? Evans... Hey, where'd Evans go?!" One of the troops whispered nervously.

"I don't know. He was standing right there a moment ago saying he would check out a rustling noise in the bushes." Said another.

"Evans!" We all yelled panicked as we scurried to find cover.

Looking in the trees, I could've sworn I saw something moving in the brush as well. Evans, who is one of our elite soldiers, seemed to vanish into thin air. One by one the troops started disappearing... Was it her? Was she stalking us and picking us apart? We started out with 10 troops; we were now down to 3. How is she doing this in broad daylight? As soon as we made it through the thick understory of the forest, we were met with a stern warning that stopped us dead in our tracks.

"STOP! Come any closer and I will end you!" Said a strong female voice that rang throughout the forest.

The troops started shooting in the direction of the voice. They ended up with daggers protruding out of their chest because of it. She was fast... I didn't even see her throw them...

"Hey! Wait, wait! I mean you no harm. I'm just here to talk to you about a common enemy. A secret organization that could possibly be involved in causing the **apocalypse.** We're on the same side!" I said as my pulse was racing, and my face was drenched in sweat.

"What do you know about the apocalypse? You have no idea what's going on. You need to leave now and never come back!" She said still cloaked among the trees.

"I am a part of the Delta region. We don't believe in the Omnis-Chip or what the government or secret organization is doing. We believe they have found a way to time travel and use the chip to control people to do their bidding."

"They are... You came up with that theory all by yourself?" She asked with a hint of sarcasm in her voice.

"Well not me alone, my faction, the Deltas started to research the chip and secret organization. We've seen photos that show shadowy figures and a woman in a hoody in pictures of prominent men and women throughout history."

"Good observation." She said as she uncloaked herself and walked towards me.

"Look, we are on the same team here." I said as I dropped my weapons and held my hands up in surrender.

"I'm not going to hurt you. I had to be sure you were not a threat. And by the goodness of your heart, I can tell you are genuinely seeking the truth."

"What do you mean, the goodness of my heart? How do you know I'm good or not lying and why are you here in the forest?" I said not trying to antagonize but to clarify her statement.

"I mean, we have a six sense or discernment and can pick up on when someone is telling the truth or has a hidden agenda. Call it divine intervention or purpose as why I am here. Ok, I am going to pull the curtain back on who I am as I fear it is already too late for mankind." She said with a distraught expression on her face.

"Too late? What do you mean?" I said concerned.

"There is a war going on behind the scenes that mankind has not completely been privy to. A war that has been going on since the beginning of man. A war between good and evil, light and dark, God and the devil. We are called sentients or sentient soldiers who are tasked to keep the balance and allow mankind to choose freely how they want to live. If the balance is off kilter or interrupted, we step in to remove the hindrance and restore the balance. The hindrance being anyone or anything that steps in the way of someone making their own decisions on how they choose to live. Not people who have influence, but people who have been manipulated by unnatural methods or unholy technology. Like the Omnis-Chip you mentioned."

"When you say we, who are you referring to? And who else would hinder mankind from making our own decisions?"

"We have many sentient soldiers, we at least did when I was still a part of the sentient corps... But we are charged to watch over mankind by *The Seer.* We're able to shift and manipulate time with our bracelets. Time travel as you call it. When we detect an abnormality in how someone is being influenced, we investigate to ensure it is on their own terms."

"Ok so y'all are like angels or something?" I said trying to wrap my head around the concept.

"Something like that. We are the good guys. And we want to ensure that **The Faithful Ones,** and the wielders of the stones, have a chance to make it to judgment day and fulfil their purpose. They are chosen leaders and vital to The Seer's plan."

"Ok this is a lot to take in... I mean if you're the 'good guys,' why did you kill all of those people? And why did you turn my squad into shish kebab back there."

"Self-defense really but killing is our last resort. I didn't kill all of your troops today, only the ones who shot at me. And though I am of sentient blood, I have gone astray and off our righteous path. You see, I allowed myself to become persuaded by a **lure** and started working with the enemy. I am responsible for creating the chip and time travel technology. I used my bracelet to create the technology and have knowledge beyond years to create more advanced tech. Thus, my hooded cloaking device I used on you and your team. It's also the hood you've seen me wear in the pictures you've just mentioned. We age slower: are way stronger, faster, and more durable than you humans. We are great in hand to hand combat as well. Though I have been in several memorable photos throughout history, I was only there to see to it that no one interfered with the work we were doing to further test the chip. The other figures in trench coats are called *Lures* or *The Persuaded.* They are the bad guys and want to see humanity perish. They feed off the disparity and anguish of mankind and want nothing more than death and destruction." She said with a look of disappointment in her eyes.

"So, who else is the enemy, and what made you go off the

beaten path?" I said not trying to pester her or sound like Christian Slater in *Interview with a Vampire.*

"Well, The Seer and I did not agree on how we should manage our prospects and engage the ones who interfered with the natural process and order of choice. I was more aggressive, and The Seer was more passive with his approach. Which angered me... This anger allowed me to become susceptible to the lures or persuaded and they were able to influence me to work for them. *The Adversary*, the enemy, was able to recruit me from that point. Now that I am free from his control, I've been on my own trying to right my wrongs in hopes of being forgiven for my transgressions."

"This is crazy! I have so many questions! I mean who are **The Faithful Ones**? What are the stones? And what is your name?!"

"My name is **Malaika**, but you can call me Mal. Though 'Lady of Death' has an interesting ring to it." She said facetiously.

"And the faithful ones and the stones; you will find out who and what they are soon enough." She said as she smiled, retrieved her daggers, and ran off through the forest turning on her concealment cloak.

As I stood there trying to further process the order of events that just occurred, I couldn't help but think about the tall, radiantly beautiful, and angelic woman that just shared her heart with me. She was well-spoken and exuded confidence in a way that showed her experience. The hoody she wore was dark gray and looked like it was made from tough fiber. Her daggers came back to her like she had magnetic gauntlets or vambraces on. They also had strange symbols or writings on the handle that looked ancient. But why me? Why did she feel comfortable enough to tell me the truth about the chip and past events? Does she know my future? Has she seen my past? And what did she mean when she said, "you will find out who and what they are soon enough?" I don't know if anyone will believe me when I tell them this; even though it confirms our theories on the chip and time travel were correct. But only time will tell what happens next...

RAT RACE

Insidiously sinister time seems to creep up from behind and cause a gamut of concern or worry as I lay awake at night and ponder my life, and how I've lived it up to this point. Time is an evil mistress that takes and takes with little reward. The witching hour begins to flower and bloom darkness that consumes my room until I can't think or sleep anymore. But just lay awake and stare into space a dark void of time the seems to burst but never shines at the seams but never gleams throughout the night. The 24 hours, 52 weeks, 365 days, and 12 months we get every year are constantly moving forward. Time isn't inherently evil in itself, but it can only be redeemed and salvaged by the moments we seize. The moments we capture like a picture in our mental camera. The good, the bad, and the ugly is all there. Locked away in a secret vault until we want to share them with family or friends. What family? What friends? I live alone in this one-bedroom apartment among the mundane. And though rhetorical, I seek answers like an oracle but do not understand the creators plan further than I can plan which is seldom past the 24 hours in which we stand or sit down. The witching hour seems to devour my hope and puts a spell on me like dope to cope with meaningless mediocrity. I toss and turn hoping one day I will learn from my past mistakes and bad choices. Go to work; come home, try to sleep and do it again, the vicious cycle goes on and on and for what? Just to get a promotion?! Just to make some corporation who doesn't really care about our wellbeing more money?! Just to waste away and achieve **success,** but what is success without sanity? The gravity of the situation is heavy and can cost us everything. The menial 9 to 5 jobs where we are just cogs in the big machine called corporate or blue-collar America. The circadian rhythm seems off beat and I can rarely sleep as I constantly compete with myself and others to stay on top, but we're just stuck. Stuck in a rut or what us intrepid labor workers like to call the **Rat Race.** We have the wheels, we have the cheese, but nothing seems to please just appease our need to feed our emotional appetite or intelligence. To feed our ego we try to create masterpieces with our lives like Van Gogh, but seldom scratch the surface of our true potential strengths. However, our weaknesses seem to amplify blaringly. The colors don't blend well and bleed through the canvas as our heart tries to find ways to be full. Our need to belong or be liked; loved better yet, is uncanny...

But what's love without pain. Pain without pleasure. Pleasure without fun. Does anyone know? Is it the butterflies we feel when we meet that special someone, we consider our soul mate? Is it the intimacy we share inside and outside of the bedroom with the same person or multiple partners, but still feel platonic at best? Whether I'm single or in a relationship I feel alone even with a warm body or warm bodies next to mine. Speaking of bodies, the bodies chopped up in my fridge will only provide nutrients for some time... Sometimes I go out of my way to lure my victims back to my place. Entice them, then rip them limb, from limb. Other times it's happenstance and we catch eyes at a glance and connect on a molecular level. Either way it makes me feel more alive... Am I serious? Maybe, maybe not... but either way I will have to go out and buy boring TV dinners after my freezer is empty to avoid emaciation. Which could be better than eating processed food with chemicals I can't pronounce. Microwaveable sustenance that barely provides nutrients but is better than eating air sandwiches of the imaginary kind. Meatloaf, Salisbury steak, Chili Mac, are kind of bland unless you add salt. Speaking of salt, let's talk about how salty I am I didn't get the promotion today. I work my fingers to the bone and expose my phalanges, and it still goes unnoticed. I still feel unappreciated...

Our existential purpose seems clouded when you repeat the same day repeatedly... and then there's the mouse trap that I put cheese on every night. How is this mouse stealing the cheese without setting off the trap? I've tried different traps and different types of cheese but can't seem to find the right one to kill this mouse. Provolone, pepper jack, Gouda, the good stuff! And this little bastard steals them all every night! I've even tried to use the Pythagorean theorem to find angles at which this nuisance could possibly take the bait from a live trap. I've triggered the trap several times to test it. It clamped down on my finger so hard I popped a blood vessel in my forehead from laughing hysterically in pain. But still no success... I even bought a cat and named him Tom. No luck with him either. I caught Tom with the trap instead of the mouse and eventually got rid of him. I feel like someone is playing a trick on me, but I'm the only one here. I live in an apartment complex, but it seems I am the only one who's ever around. Most days I avoid the mirror as I don't like looking at my reflection. I am starting to look scruffy and pale like a vampire. Reminiscent of when I first saw the movie *Candyman*, I tend to walk around not knowing what I look like for days. When I go to work, I commute by train or bus so no need for personal transportation. My coworkers think I'm nuts for how I think and conversate, but what can I say, I'm a realist who is quite pessimistic. I can't remember much about my past, and only know about my future, which is more labor work and feeling like a mindless zombie... speaking of mindless zombie, my urge to feed on brains is rising once again...

"Wow, this flesh bag is really depressing... I don't know how much more I can take of this."

"I hear you Rod; these flesh bags are a piece of work let me tell you. I had one the other day that tried to escape the simulation by running up the walls. We had to zap him back into reality."

"Man, I wish I was there to see that Jerry hahaha. I mean, it's a cryin shame that our hard-earned tax dollars are funding this rehabilitation program for these filthy wads of meat. It is entertaining watching them sometimes though. This guy I'm watching now is like *Shakespeare* mixed with *Hannibal Lecter* in how he expresses himself. Too bad he was a serial killing piece of crap. He could have been something otherwise… But they don't pay me to think, just to run test and monitor cognitive functions while they are in these simulations so what do I know…"

"They're all criminals on death row anyway, so why try to rehabilitate them Rod?"

"Well, they want to test to see if this program works or not so they can try it out in the real world. And since they're going to die anyway, if we lose some in the process, no harm no foul. I tell you what though, I'm not letting myself nor my babies go anywhere near this thing. If they need rehabilitation, we got the belt or obstacle course for that you know what I'm sayin."

"Yeah I hear you. And don't you have like 35 kids now?"

"Yeah, so what Jerry, it's been a busy season if you know what I mean hahaha. And besides, what do you think I'm pulling all this over time for huh, shiggles? My kids gotta eat!"

"I hear you hahaha… And speaking of eating, how'd you like the mousetrap I added to the simulation?"

"Pretty pretentious don't you think? I'm just kiddin, I thought it was freakin hilarious making this fleshy turd freak out every night hahaha! Woah, watch the tail…"

"Sorry about that Rod, didn't see it laying there. Well, I'm clocking out for the night. My wheel is in the shop so I'm riding home with Morty. Enjoy 'observing' your fleshbag."

"Yeah there's never a dull moment in corporate science. Ok you two furballs, be safe. See you in the AM, where it's back to the 9 to 5 grind of trying to take over the world..."

"Sounds like a plan. See you then!"

THE SHOWING

It was a warm muggy day in April. The humid Kentucky air whisked through my fingers as I rolled the window down to feel the Southern breeze. My husband and I were looking for a new home we could start a family in. It's been a journey trying to find an affordable home in good condition, but the market for home mortgage rates are at an all-time low, so we had to capitalize.

"Hey honey, turn the music down will you, I just got a text from the realtor saying he may be a little late to the showing today. He also said he left the door unlocked so we can go right in."

"Sorry babe, you know I like to jam when my music is on. And that's fine. Seems like this one is in **BFE**. Are you sure you want to check it out?" He said looking perturbed.

"Yes, I still want to see it! The pictures looked great on-line... it has a lake in the back, plenty of land, and more than enough room to start our family."

"That's fine; but just remember, if we get lost, stranded, or brutally murdered out here, this was a house you saw as an option to live in." He said as he snickered under his breath.

"That's not funny you jerk!" I said hitting him in his arm while laughing.

"Just playing. I thought the pictures of the house looked great as well. Since we have some time to kill before we get there, let's play a little game. What's your favorite scary movie to watch?! I know we talked about this before but also name how you would die in that movie." He said in a creepy sadistic voice."

"But honey, it's only April, Halloween is a long way from now. Do I have to play?" I said not in the mood to play any silly road trip games.

"Yes! C'mon love, it'll be fun! See look, I'll go first. My favorite 'horror' movie to watch is *Night of the Living Dead.* 'They're coming to get you Barbara,' George Romero was a genius! Greg Nicotero is another juggernaut when it comes to zombie movies, make up, and special effects! And I would probably die like Tony Todd in the 1990 remake and get shot by some prick and turn into a zombie. See, it's that simple... now it's your turn!"

"Ok, but zombie movies give me the creeps... I like *Dawn of the Dead* and *Zombieland*, but that one gave me the chills watching it. I guess if I had to choose, I would pick *Friday the 13th*. **Jason Voorhees** rocks! Part III and Part VI are my favorite out of the series. Jason X was fun too. Jason in space, how crazy can you get! But of course, I would get wrecked and hacked into pieces in classic Jason fashion."

"Nice! Good choice babe! See that wasn't so bad right?! When we get back home, we should do a horror movie marathon!" He said as he smiled from ear to ear.

"Yeah that was pretty cool. But I feel like you're trying to freak me out before we get there... How much longer anyway?" I said getting a little anxious to see if the house was a contender in our search for refuge.

"Not much further. I think the GPS has us a little lost though, so we'll have to go off of the handwritten directions from the realtor. And I'm not trying to 'freak you out,' just wanted to show that we both have an affinity for horror movies and have one more thing we connect on."

"Awww, that's sweet hun. I guess we can play again if you want."

As we made our way to see the house, we encountered a long winding road riddled with potholes. They were so bad, it felt like our vehicle was going to fall apart as we crawled steadily along. The location was secluded and definitely in **BFE** as my husband stated before. There was an ENTER AT YOUR OWN RISK sign on one of the trees while we were traveling down the jagged road. This caused me to feel even more trepidatious about this abandoned house in the woods... As we finally made our way to the house, it looked different from the pictures online. I was a bit nauseous from our bumpy ride down the treacherous road of doom. The driveway was cragged and had us walking sideways to get to the front door. The stench of moldy lake water and dead animal carcasses filled the air. Not sure if this would be an ideal place to raise a family...

"Hey babe, this place sucks! Can we leave now?" My husband said in a serious yet joking tone.

"No, not yet! We drove all this way and haven't seen the inside..." I said giving him the 'get your life together look.'

"Ok, whatever you say my love... Hey, what's up with that random truck on the hill over there? You think it belongs to the last victims that came to see this house?" He said facetiously.

"I don't know, but it is a little weird."

Once we shimmied down the steep hill that is the driveway, we came to the front door that was slightly opened.

"The realtor said he would leave the door open; do you want to go inside or stay out here and wait to be massacred." He said as he laughed emphatically.

"You are being a real butthole you know that?! It's starting to get annoying... Can we just look at the house and be on our merry way if it is completely off the table?" I said angrily as I walked into the house.

"Sorry babe, I'll be more serious going forward. Cross my heart, hope to die, stick **Jason Voorhees** machete in my eye."

I can't stand him sometimes, but he always knows how to make me laugh and It's hard to stay mad at him... As we began our journey through the house, I noticed we didn't have any cellphone signal out here. That was kind of concerning... My husband and I tend to venture in different directions when we're viewing a home. We've seen a lot of homes in our journey to find one that best fits our needs. It's been a struggle, but we will keep looking until the right one turns up. From the looks of this place, the search will most likely continue... The house was dilapidated on the inside and had an overwhelming gas smell to it. It doesn't look like it's been lived in for some time. The owner was out of state and was just looking to get rid of it, so we could get a good deal on it if we put in an offer. The house was definitely a fixer-upper but had some potential even still. The lake was nice and came fully stocked with fish. There was 10 acres of land that would be great for farming or to build on. It had nice paths that we could walk down in the evenings or early morning for meditation and conversation. And with it being so run down, I'm sure we could put in a low bid and use the rest of the money for renovations.

"Babe! Come quick! You're not going to believe this!" He yelled from the hallway.

Startled, I hurried into the hallway towards what appeared to be the bedroom to see if he was ok.

"What is it Honey! You ok?!"

As I rushed into the room, I couldn't believe my eyes. Staring at us on a wall, was a huge mural of no other than **Jason Voorhees**...

"Check this out! How awesome is this! It's like the home-owners knew you were a huge Jason fan!" He said ecstatic about the mural.

I on the other hand was freaked out by it... Though I'm a huge fan of Jason, I don't think I want to wake up to him in my hallway every morning...

"Yeah sweetheart, but isn't it strange that the owner painted a mural of a serial killer on their wall?"

"No, he's an imaginary movie monster, they are probably just really big fans of the movies that's all. I'm starting to like this house a little more now. Let's check out the bedrooms!"

It was a 4-bedroom 3-bathroom house with a jacuzzi in the main bedroom which was nice. The bedrooms were a decent size and I did like the living room and patio. The odd thing was, there were bullet casings everywhere on the ground...

"Hey honey, do you see these bullet casings on the ground? What do you think happened here?"

"I don't know, but you would think the realtor would clean this place up before showing it to anyone... I know it's an 'as is house,' but this is ridiculous!"

"Take a look at this, do you see that glare in the top corner by the front door. Looks like a camera... ok I think it's time to go." I said with an eerie feeling and chill bumps on my arm.

"Yeah I'm with you on that babe." He said looking rattled.

As we made our way to the door, we heard the Jason whisper theme playing faintly in the background. The C*h ch ch; ah ah ah* sound had us both scared out of our minds. And if you knew the real meaning which was K*i ki ki; ma ma ma,* you would totally crap your pants at this point... What was going on? Was our realtor trying to play a trick on us or was it the owner playing games?

"What was that?!" He said frantically.

"It's the Jason whisper theme that's played right before he goes on a killing spree."

"I thought so but didn't want you to think I was still messing with you."

When we tried to open the door, it was locked from the outside and blocked by something heavy.

"Hey! This isn't funny... stop messing around whoever you are! I have a gun on me, and I'll use it if I have to!" He yelled through the door.

"Who are you screaming at honey?! They can obviously see and hear us whoever they are. Let's not panic all the way yet. We need to go outside and try to get a signal to call the realtor or the police." I said trying to keep my composure the best I could.

"You're right babe... I'm just pissed off that someone would pull this type of prank on people trying to buy a house from them. The mural was cool, but the bullet shells and creepy Jason music is a bit much."

"Though I'm a fan, I agree wholeheartedly."

Soon as we ran to the back door, we were met with a barrage of gunshots that had us diving on the floor.

"I'm hit!" My husband screeched in agony as he grabbed his

arm while rolling on the floor.

"Oh my God! Honey are you okay?!" I said screaming at the top of my lungs and worried for our lives.

"It hurts! but I'm ok... Just stay down and don't move!"

Bullets ricocheted throughout the house and dismantled the walls and appliances that were staged there. If we make it out alive, I am definitely leaving a negative review online... But seriously, we may die, and I may not experience the joys of motherhood and having a family. We have to do what it takes to get through this. We've seen enough scary movies to know what not to do to survive. We also know that the killer always reveals themselves, so we will weigh our options when that happens. They also have to reload at some point; when they do, we will make a run for it and try to find help.

"They stopped shooting, now's our chance to get out of here! I'll be able to manage as I think the bullet went through my shoulder." He said wincing in pain.

We were able to run through the back door and down the stairs through nearby woods. We did our best to look for traps and tried not to randomly trip on imaginary shrubbery. They started to shoot at us again while we were ducking, dodging, and running as fast as we could to cover.

"Wait wait, let me catch my breath for a moment."

"Are you ok honey?! You're bleeding pretty badly." I said applying pressure to his wound with a makeshift bandage made from his shirt.

"I'm ok, just need a moment... I'm starting to feel a little light-headed and fleeing through these woods like we're in a scary movie isn't helping. We have to find someone quick. But since we're in the middle of nowhere, that may take a while..."

"I know I was trying to be optimistic with this house, but it took a drastic turn for the worst. I'm sorry sweetheart." I said as tears streamed down my face.

"Hey hey, it's not your fault love. You didn't know we would be hunted like animals out here by raging psychopaths. Although, I did warn you that strange things happen in the boonies. We are kind of in our own horror movie which beats watching it on TV, so that's cool." He said as he chuckled a bit trying to make me smile.

"Yeah, I think we are holding up pretty good considering most people would be dead by now in the movies." I said holding him up as we prepared to journey further to find help.

"Wait, do you hear that?"

"Hear what?!"

"That rustling sound... get down!"

My heart was pounding as we laid there as quietly as possible behind a fallen log.

Ch ch ch; ah ah ah... Ch ch ch...

The Jason whisper eerily reverberated through the dense forest. We couldn't see anyone, but we could hear the sound of silence and the terrifying whisper piercing the humid air. It was almost night fall as this was a late showing booked by our realtor. We were paralyzed by fear at this moment but had to move quick as my husband was still bleeding profusely.

"Ok babe, we're going to have to make a run for it. I'm bleeding bad and don't know how much longer I can hold out without medical attention." He said in a low labored voice.

"Ok, we'll make a run for it on 3... 1, 2, 3!"

I hoisted my husband up and we made a beeline towards the nearest tree. I felt a burning sensation in my right leg and fell to the ground. I think I've been shot! I have to get up and keep moving. At that moment, I saw a bright flash of light and then nothingness... I was knocked out cold...

When I came to, my husband and I were sitting side by side handcuffed in chairs in front of a pentagram. The pentagram was on the floor and we were surrounded by 6 people wearing nightmarishly deformed devil masks. 3 guys and 3 females... They all had knives, and one had a machete. Their guns were on the floor by the far wall, but still accessible. My husband wasn't moving. I screamed his name, but no response.

"Uh oh, we have ourselves a screamer. We love screamers... don't we guys!" Said the guy holding the machete.

"Yeah, these screaming sheep make this worthwhile!" Said another guy taunting us.

My husband started to come to at this time.

"Are you ok honey?!"

"Yeah, yeah I'm ok..." He said slowly regaining consciousness.

"Stay with me sweetheart, we're going to make it through this." I said trying to give us a false sense of hope.

"I don't know, they look pretty evil... who would have thought when we woke up today, we would be fighting for our lives in some run-down dump in the woods." He said still trying to put a smile on my face.

"This is not how I planned this day would go either. I'm sorry babe..." I said in tears.

"Stop apologizing, it's not your fault. If we don't make it out alive. Just know that I love you with all of my heart and I'm thankful for the time we've shared." He said as he leaned closer to me.

"I can't keep it a secret any longer knowing we may not have a lot of time; I'm pregnant honey. You're going to be a father..." I said with a smile on my face trying to sound happy.

"What?! Your joking right? I'm going to be a father?! I'm going to be a father!" He said hopping up in down with joy.

After I told my husband the good news, one of the evil bastards took their knife and slit his throat. There was blood everywhere... I sat there in shock for a moment, as I was drenched in his blood... "You monsters! How could you!" I cried erratically. "I just told him he was going to be a father, and you took that away from me!" I yelled still screaming in anguish.

"There's just something about feeling the life leave someone's body while using a blade opposed to a gun. It's almost poetic..." He said slowly with a raspy voice and sneering tone.

"But hey, that's great news for us... Two souls for the price of one!" Said the guy with the machete as they stood there mockingly.

I'm sure the tall, brooding, butcher with the machete was the leader of this satanic cult. I assumed they were devil worshippers with the pentagram on the ground, and deformed masks they wore. They dressed in all black and looked like adrenaline junkies trying to score their next fix. The girls had dark nail polish, tight faded jeans, gothic tops, and spiked bracelets. The guys also had spiked bracelets, spiked collars, leather work boots, and ripped coveralls on. This was something out of my worst nightmare...

"The sacrifice will be fitting this time around. We hope it's fully accepted by the dark lord. You know we love to hunt people for fun; but long life, wealth, and prosperity is an added bonus." He said as they started laughing loudly.

They all formed a circle around the pentagram and began chanting something in a disturbing language, one I've never heard before. They were positioned at each point of the star and had their eyes closed while they chanted vigorously. One thing they didn't account for, is that I grew up with brothers who were MMA fighters, and a father that taught me how to escape dangerous situations such as these. I already scoped out my surroundings and knew my plan of attack. I can dislocate my thumbs to get out of handcuffs and use them as a weapon with precision. I can also shoot any weapon known to man with pinpoint accuracy. They picked the wrong one, and will pay for what they've done to us... The guy with the machete, grabbed my hair and pulled my head back to expose my neck. He put the sharp blade against my throat, looked me in the eyes and said:

"Any last words love?"

"Yeah, how would you die in a scary movie?" I said as I freed my hands from the cuffs and kicked the chair backwards.

While he was stunned by what I did; I upkicked the machete out of his hand, knocked him to the ground with a single leg sweep, and stabbed him in the neck with the handcuffs.

"She stabbed me! Get her..." He gurgled to his minions as they snapped out of their trance.

I made a mad dash for the AR-15 by the wall and shredded them all like swiss cheese… The leader was crawling on the floor spitting up blood. I turned him over and took the mask off. I didn't recognize his face, but his voice sounded familiar. We spoke once before. It was the owner of the house…

"Why did you do this to us?! How many other families have you ruined because you wanted to make a deal with the devil?!" I said as I kicked him repeatedly.

"Cause I can." He said laughing while gurgling up more blood.

"Ok… before I chop you up into little pieces and feed you to the fish, how did you know my favorite movie monster was **Jason Voorhees** from *Friday the 13th?*" I said genuinely curious about it.

"Huh, Jason is my favorite too. I rigged the house up to pay homage and to have some fun. What a coincidence… You know we may have been on the same side in another life." He said as I started lopping off his appendages starting at his ankles.

Bloody, broken, and still hazy about the order of events that just occurred, I sat by my husband's lifeless body stroking his hair and balling my eyes out. I then heard radio static from one of the killer's bags. It was a walkie talkie. I picked it up to hear it more clearly.

"Hello, come in. Are you there? Is it done? Don't play around with me Damien. I delivered as promised." The voice said as I turned the volume up louder.

"Damien?! Where are you?!" He said urgently.

Since there were girls in this twisted crew, I thought he

wouldn't notice a difference if I responded.

"Hello; yeah Damien is in pieces about something right now, but he said he has your money and needs you to get here asap." I said trying to sound calm yet sadistic.

"Ok, I am not that far out. I'll be there shortly."

As I waited for this sorry excuse of a human being to show up, I thought it would be best to return the favor and scare him to death before I actually killed him. Yes, I was at that point... They took everything from me; they all have to pay... First, I need to kill the cameras then set the stage for the next scene. I moved Damien's decapitated body closer to the door so the realtor could see him first, then put his mask on. At this point, I don't care why the realtor set us up. It was obviously for money... but people who would craft such a nefarious plan, don't deserve to live...

"Hello, where are you guys?! Why is it so dark in here? Woah!" He said as he slipped on the blood by the door.

He screamed in terror as he saw all the blood and Damien's headless corpse laying on the floor. He ran out of the house scared for his life. I followed him at a slow yet steady pace. Covered in blood, I chased him through the woods, wielding the machete, and quietly whispered:

Ch ch ch; ah ah ah... Ki ki ki; ma ma ma... until I blacked out and the rage took over.

PASSING THROUGH

Have you ever felt like you were going in circles or felt trapped in a loop and couldn't move forward? This is how it's been for me and my family for a few years now. My life has been in shambles since I came back from the war... I can't seem to keep a steady job; I'm short tempered with everyone including my wife, and I've thought about suicide on numerous occasions because of it. My PTSD, anxiety, and depression have crippled my way of life, and though I get compensated for it, I'm still tormented by the nightmares and ghosts from my past. Every Tuesday for the past couple of months, like clockwork I've been seeing my psychiatrist to help with my mental struggles. The medication I'm on has me feeling lethargic, but it has helped me manage my mental health challenges some. I still have panic attacks, night terrors, and horrible nightmares that literally have me fighting for my life though. I try to do my best to power through it, but it has been challenging to cope with as of late. I can still hear and feel the bullets like it was yesterday... I started sleeping on the couch again, so I don't mistake my wife for the enemy and attack her. I haven't done it yet, but came close a few times in the past...

I'm thankful she's still with me after all the hell I put her through. Thankful I have a loving supportive wife that is still with me through the trials and tribulations we've had on this journey together. My sons still call me their hero; well, after *Spiderman* and the *Hulk* that is. But they always tell me and their mom they want to be like me when they grow up. They're four and six years old so that is to be expected. It makes me feel good knowing that, but it's hard to fully accept when I look introspectively on the things I've done and seen... They don't know their father has killed people for a living. Though it was a part of my job to do so, I'm haunted by the faces of everyone I've pulled the trigger on and dropped. Did they all die? Was it murder? Or was it me just doing what I had to do to serve my country? I had to protect and serve my troops and did what was necessary for us to survive. Doesn't make it any easier to live with though... Secretly, I've also done some mercenary work to help track down victims of sexual abuse and sex trafficking, but that still didn't keep my demons at bay...

Being a born-again believer that has faith in my Lord and Savior Jesus Christ, I've sought help through prayer and support from my church. I guess I wanted confirmation that all my sins could truly be forgiven or washed away by praying and pleading the blood; like the old hymnal by Robert Lowry suggests. But I've had a really hard time forgiving myself for the things I've done as of late...

"Hello Mr. Myers, how's it going?"

"It's going ok Doc, I guess." I said as I shook my psychiatrists' hand and tried to get comfortable.

Those leather couches have always been hard to get used to. My last doctor I cursed out... I felt like he was antagonizing me and knew how to push my buttons. Patronizing your patients will never go well especially people who suffer from PTSD. My new doc seems to be pretty cool and understanding. Doesn't patronize or get on my nerves as much as my previous doctor, so that's good. Our first couple of sessions were rough though. It was challenging for me to open up initially as I hated feeling vulnerable in front of a complete stranger... In time, I learned to just let my thoughts flow and be as real as possible with the severity of my issues. He seemed genuine and was patient with me, so I started sharing more about my past and my triggers.

"Just ok? Let's talk about it. We've made good progress in our last session and really centralized or identified what the root cause of your PTSD is. Tell me what's been going on lately though." He said as he prepared to scribble on his notepad.

"Well Doc, I've been having really bad nightmares lately. You know, night terrors that feel so real, that I wake up not knowing where I am or if it's real or not. I started sleeping on the couch as I fear I may hurt my wife or boys if they startled me. I also been hearing voices and seeing things... it has me feeling like I'm in an endless loop of a NIGHTMARE ON ELM ST movie, and *Freddy Krueger* is around the corner waiting to disembowel me..."

"I hate to hear that you are dealing with that Mr. Myers. You have made great progress in this area since we've been meeting, and I want to get to the root of this resurgence of nightmares or emotions you're experiencing. Have you been taking your prescription for anxiety and sleeping aides regularly?"

"I may have missed a few dosages on the anxiety meds as they hinder my sexual performance and enjoyment, which just makes me even more depressed. The night terror meds make me feel more angry, homicidal even, so I don't know if I should continue taking those." I said a little embarrassed by my answers.

"We can look at other medications and dosages to find the right one for you. Definitely don't want to aggravate your symptoms or make them any worse. Tell me about the voices and nightmares you've been having. If you can remember them; I want to write down specific elements of the imagery to determine if there is significance regarding your trauma."

"You sure Doc? They're pretty intense and graphic to say the least..."

"Yes please. I've heard it all, and it will help me understand how to best provide consultation for you specifically. Don't worry, this is strictly confidential." He said as he scribbled some more on his notepad.

Not sure what he was writing, but he does that a lot... kind of puts me on edge like I am being observed for some science project or something...

"Ok Doc. Well first off, the voices I hear sometimes sound kind and helpful. The others sound evil and demonic... They tell me to do things that I don't want to repeat." I said fidgeting in the chair.

"That's fine, you don't have to repeat them. Just tell me this, if it's ok, do they ever tell you to hurt yourself or anyone else?"

"Yes, all the time... I guess the demons of our past, catch up with us eventually..."

"I see. You say you own guns correct?" He said jotting down notes.

"I do, but I'm in enough control not to use them unless I absolutely have to for protection. Besides, my wife keeps them locked up and has the key hid just in case. I'm a lethal killing machine without them as I know several forms of martial arts and Brazilian Jiu Jitsu." I said somewhat jokingly.

"That's good to hear you have accountability when it comes to your wife. She is definitely instrumental in your therapy and mental health progression."

"Yeah, I love my wife. I've put her through so much, but she is still with me. I am truly a blessed man." I said as I started tearing up.

"I have tissues on the desk if you need them."

"No I'm good. See, this is why I didn't want to talk to you about this stuff. I hate crying! I hate being vulnerable around people. Especially one's I don't know like that..." I said wiping my eyes dry.

"You're totally fine. I am here for you. Sometimes, it's best to cry and share your story or challenges with a complete stranger. They are less likely to judge you. Other times not so much as they may take advantage of you and tell you to stop your yammering. My sessions will always be the former." He said trying to make me laugh and make me more comfortable.

"Yeah, I hear you Doc." I said sniffling and chuckling at the same time.

"We don't have to deep dive into everything right away. Do you feel comfortable telling me about the dreams you've been having?"

"Yeah, I'll tell you." I said as I started tapping my feet nervously.

"Ok take your time."

"Well... I've had some trippy dreams as of late. The one's I remember have certain details that stick out to me in regard to the war. One where I was stuck in a virtual rehabilitation program being analyzed like a rat in a cage. Another where my wife and I were house shopping, but we were kidnapped, and she killed the ones that held us captive. I actually died in that one, but she scared the crap out of me for days after that. Had me sleeping with one eye open and everything... We both love horror movies, so it made sense... I even had a nightmare where I saw myself and one of my childhood friends get killed by the police after a traffic stop. It was weird as the timeline was off and I felt like I was in another person's body... But the one that scared me the most because it seemed so real, was where I turned into a monster and devoured anyone that came close to me while traveling through this lonely town I've never seen before."

"Interesting.... The dreams or nightmares seem to be unique. Other than fear, do you remember how you felt during each one?"

"Scared out of my mind! Each dream was like an out of body experience, but I remember everything vividly. Especially the one where I morphed into a murderous beast salivating for its next victim."

"Tell me about that one. Seems like that's the dream that provoked the most emotion, physically and psychologically."

"Yes sir, that one still bothers me til this day. But it starts where I get off a bus at night. Before I get off, the bus driver asks me 'what will I be doing while I'm in town.' I told him, nothing, just **passing through**... I don't know where I was headed or what town I was in, but I started walking aimlessly down this vacant strip. While I was walking, I passed several stores I vaguely remember, but all the streetlights were off and there were no people around at first. There's a smell of sea salt and boiled peanuts in the air so there seemed to be a carnival nearby. I remember hearing an eerily somber melody playing softly in the background. As I was walking, I took a turn into a dingy dark alley where I was followed by 3 shadowy figures. When I came to the end of the alley way, I was overtaken by them all... I could literally feel myself fighting in my sleep. My wife told me I was punching and kicking uncontrollably during this nightmare. The worst part was after I was overtaken by the shadow creatures, I emerged a creature myself. I had ravenous fangs, butchering claws, and eyes as dark as sin. I then let out the most gut-wrenching growl and scream that felt evil and could wake up the dead. It felt like I was awake at this moment, but I was still asleep." I said as I got chills recalling the events.

That wasn't even the worst part. After I growled like an enraged animal, I saw lights and a Ferris wheel. I raced towards the noise and families laughing and enjoying the festivities. I began to impale and mutilate anyone that was close to me... I tried to wake up so many times during that nightmare, but I couldn't do it...

There was so much blood and gore that a slasher movie director would be jealous. My new doctor was even there... I ripped him to shreds... I'm not a bad person, and I don't want him to think I'm completely crazy. So I'll keep that part to myself. Some of the horrors of war seem to keep manifesting themselves in different aspects of my life. Even in my dreams...

"Sounds like your past keeps following you and wants you to be someone you are not any longer or someone you've never been. When you turned into this monster, what do you do after that?"

"I don't really want to talk about it Doc. It gets fuzzy after that anyway, and I finally snap out of it and wake up. I've had issues with remembering certain things as well. Maybe some other time."

"Ok no rush. Just want to further understand and try to analyze your dreams more thoroughly. People who have PTSD due to trauma caused by war or any other terrible event, could have multiple triggers that effect mood, attitude, and mental stability all around. You've told me some of the things you had to do being deployed before, and I don't want to rehash that. I do want to reevaluate your medication to see if we can try a different dosage and gauge its effectiveness."

"You know Doc, I've killed a lot of bad guys; well people who I thought were bad guys. And some that were in the wrong place at the wrong time, but I did it because I was serving my country. I regret a lot of things, but I don't regret serving. It was my job as an Army Ranger and Sergeant to follow orders, carry out missions, and ensure all my troops came out alive. The less casualties of war the better, but I lost some good men out there... one of which was my best friend. I blame myself for his death as I was in charge of his safety as my soldier. I let him down... Sometimes I feel like it should have been me that jumped on that bomb... But several tours to Afghanistan and Iraq can take its toll on anyone. And I believe these nightmares are just another extension of that... I'll never live a normal life. I've come to terms with that a long time ago, but I want some sense of normalcy for my wife and kids' sake... Hey Doc, you ever heard of the *Omnis-Chip?* I ask because I had a dream where we were in a post-apocalyptic world that had time traveling angels, and a chip that could make people happy as well as kill them if they got out of line or served their purpose." I said hoping to not sound too crazy.

"Omnis-Chip? No sir, I don't think I have... You said you had a dream about that as well?"

"Yep, it was surreal. A chip like that could revolutionize the medical industry as well as cause a mutiny if it fell into the wrong hands..."

"I hear you Mr. Myers, that would be something else. Could you give me a moment while I review your notes and speak with our pharmacist about your medication further?" He said as he seemed a little shaken up by what I told him.

"Sure thing Doc, take your time."

"Hello sir, we may have a problem... I have a patient here named Rick L Myers who just told me he had a dream about the **Omnis-Chip.** Do you think it's her? Do you think he's chosen? How do you want me to proceed?! Ok; uh huh. Understood sir. I'll get right on it. I'll have a status report for you soon."

"Appreciate the wait Mr. Myers."

"Please, just call me Rick. We've been through this before." I said as we both shared a laugh.

"Well, I have a new dosage and medication we can try to help with your night terrors and anxiety."

"Great! What's it called? Probably another long name I can't pronounce."

"Well, why don't you just follow me this way and we'll discuss it further."

"Sounds good. And Doc, thanks for everything..."

"My pleasure Rick, just want to do my part to help you on your journey. Thank you for your service to our country. We're going to figure this out, sooner or later..."

AFTERWORD

Short Stories of Modern Times Past is a graphic depiction of life from the point of view of an Army veteran riddled with battle scars; physically and mentally. The story sets up a bigger universe where things are not always what they seem... A world where time travel is possible, powers are real, and warriors come from all walks of life. These warriors are chosen for a higher purpose. Rick plays a part in this purpose, but only time will tell how significant... Though most events that occurred in this book are fictional, how close do you think we are to some of the future events happening in our lifetime? Looking at everything that is happening in the world today, it seems as though some events are closer than they appear. My goal when I write my stories is to first entertain my readers, but also to encourage you to open your imagination to different possibilities. I was inspired to write this book based off my own experiences and challenges as an Army veteran. It then morphed into something bigger than I expected, thanks to you, the reader!

"The best thing about the future is that it comes one day at a time."

-Abraham Lincoln

ABOUT THE AUTHOR

A.l. King

A.L. KING is an author of upcoming Fiction, Short Stories, and Syfy Thrillers. He is from Hampton Virginia and has been writing literary works for years. He recently published his first comic book/short story titled "The Indubitable World of Super Clutz." The concept of Super Clutz was drawn and written when he was 8 years old.  With the help and inspiration of his little daughter, KING wanted to bring the parody character back to life.

They began to work on the comic book series again towards the end of 2019. Being a comic book lover himself, KING wanted to create a character that was entertaining, but also one that readers could relate to. KING is also working on adventure books and short stories that deal with romance, action, mystery, Syfy thrillers, and societal issues. His new installment "Short Stories of Modern Times Past" is a dark, gritty, introspective look into the life of a young soldier named Rick Myers, who served in the Army. Rick is trying to find his way through the traumas he suffered during war. KING took a different more mature approach to his writing style to bring this story to life. If you would like exclusive content on upcoming stories by A.L. KING, please follow our social media pages and join our email list below. Thanks again for reading!

Email: authoralking3@gmail.com
Website: authoralking.wordpress.com
Facebook: authoralking3
Instagram: @a.l.king3
Twitter: @AuthorALKING3

BOOKS IN THIS SERIES

Short Stories of Modern Times Past

"Short Stories of Modern Times Past" is a dark, gritty, introspective look into the life of a young soldier named Rick Myers, who served in the Army. Rick is trying to find his way through the traumas he suffered during war. KING took a different more mature approach to his writing style to bring this story to life.

The Rock, The Marne, And The Soldier's Heart

The Rock, The Marne, and The Soldier's Heart is a short story about a young soldier who has just enlisted into the Army to escape his troubled past. It is a story about love, romance, determination, and what lengths a person is willing to go to find their purpose.

Though the characters are fictional, some of the story was influenced by KING's own personal experience while he served in the military. This story is one of several short stories KING plans on releasing in 2020. The short story book will be titled "Short Stories of Modern Times Past." This book will include stories that have the following: romance, action, drama, suspense, thrills, and eerie plot twists that will keep you on the edge of your seat! Stay tuned for more details!

Printed in Great Britain
by Amazon